Prettyboy
Must Die

Also by Kimberly Reid

My Own Worst Frenemy

Creeping with the Enemy

Sweet 16 to Life

Guys, Lies & Alibis

Perfect Liars

Prettyboy
Must Die

KIMBERLY REID

**TOR
TEEN**

A Tom Doherty Associates Book

New York

PRETTYBOY MUST DIE

Copyright © 2018 by Kimberly Reid

A Tor Teen Book
Published by Tom Doherty Associates
175 Fifth Avenue
New York, NY 10010

www.tor-forge.com

Tor® is a registered trademark of Macmillan Publishing Group, LLC.

Library of Congress Cataloging-in-Publication Data

Names: Reid, Kim, 1965– author.
Title: Prettyboy must die / Kimberly Reid.
Description: First edition. | New York : Tor Teen, 2018. | "A Tom Doherty
    Associates Book."
Identifiers: LCCN 2017039669 (print) | LCCN 2017053238 (ebook) |
    ISBN 978-0-7653-9087-5 (hardcover) | ISBN
    978-0-7653-9089-9 (ebook)
Subjects: | CYAC: Spies—Fiction. | Hackers—Fiction. | High
    schools—Fiction. | Schools—Fiction. | Assassins—Fiction. | United
    States. Central Intelligence Agency—Fiction.
Classification: LCC PZ7.R27235 (ebook) | LCC PZ7.R27235
    Pre 2018 (print) | DDC [Fic]—dc23
LC record available at https://lccn.loc.gov/2017039669

Our books may be purchased in bulk for promotional, educational, or business use. Please contact your local bookseller or the Macmillan Corporate
and Premium Sales Department at 1-800-221-7945, extension 5442, or by
email at MacmillanSpecialMarkets@macmillan.com.

First Edition: February 2018

Printed in the United States of America

0 9 8 7 6 5 4 3 2 1

*To book lovers—this wouldn't be
nearly as much fun without you.*

Acknowledgments

Books are not made without help from people who love and understand them, and I'm lucky to know a few. I am so fortunate that my editor, Bess Cozby, believed I was the right person to tell Jake's story (and Peter's!). Thank you for all of your work helping me to turn an idea into an adventure. I am also grateful to everyone at Tor Teen who helped Bess bring this story to young readers.

Being an author is an unpredictable roller-coaster ride of a career, so I'm glad my agent, Kristin Nelson, has been my one constant over the years.

Even in fiction, a bit of the writer goes into a book. I so appreciate all the people, places, and experiences that shaped me into a storyteller, but I'm especially glad for the people, my family and friends. You are the most important part.

Prettyboy
Must Die

The Middle of Nowhere, Eastern Ukraine | Spring Break

When I arrive at the compound, it's still early enough that the sun hasn't burned off last night's frost. There is no heat in this ancient beater of a delivery car, so I'm glad for the extra shirt under my hoodie, though I wish I'd remembered gloves. I stop under the bare branches of a huge maple tree just outside the gate and rub my hands together for warmth.

There is more activity than usual for this time of morning. Women are piling large suitcases into the trunks of several cars. A repurposed, probably stolen, military cargo truck is being loaded with wooden crates so heavy they require a very large man on each corner. On my way here, two cars blew by me heading for town, probably the first wave of criminals trying to make their escape. We hadn't anticipated they'd begin moving so soon, but I'm not worried about them. They won't get very far. I just hope those escapees don't include the person I'm after.

I scan the compound for any sign of him, though I have no idea what he even looks like. The men nearly drop one of the crates they're loading, and my heart almost stops. After the time I've spent getting to know this place and the people who own it, I know what's inside those crates, even if I never learned where the cargo is headed. Since they're using precious time to load it onto trucks and move it out of the compound, it must be some pretty valuable, and destructive, loot.

I grab the box from the back seat and head for the compound's entrance, the scent of garlicky sausages and oniony potato cakes making my empty stomach growl. My job here was intelligence-gathering—getting the layout of the compound, the number of people inside, number and position of civilians, maybe eavesdrop on a plan or two—while pretending to be a food runner from the lone restaurant in the nearest village, twenty minutes away.

With the information I gathered by watching the compound, we could have raided the place days ago, but we were waiting for one major player in the operation to return. He'd decided to up and leave a few days after I arrived, which had us worried he was onto me. Taking the compound without him would mean he might pop up again in a few months, running his own business somewhere more difficult to find, like a cave in deepest Afghanistan or a yurt in remotest Mongolia. So we waited.

But Pavlo Marchuk finally obliged us four hours ago, lured back to the compound by a job promotion, under the cover of darkness. Dude ought to know better than anyone that darkness hasn't been an effective cover since World War II and the invention of night-vision technology. Being here makes him an easy target for my people. For a lot of people, really—every nation-state he ever sold illegal weapons to. He knows they're coming for him.

I'm hoping that this knowledge and Pavlo's arrival are

the reasons for this sudden decision to move out, and not because they know who I really am. I still have important work to do.

I've been delivering food every day for two weeks now, but instead of the usual drill—patting me down and checking my packages before I enter—the guard just waves me on through, too busy reading papers attached to a clipboard to bother with me. He doesn't question my earlier-than-usual arrival, doesn't even ask to hold my phone until my business in the compound is done, a requirement since day one. I take all of these things as a good sign. Distracted workers—and a camera—will make my work easier.

Officially, my job ended a few hours ago with Marchuk's return to the compound. When my boss finds out I'm here today, which she will because my people are watching—we're always watching—I'll tell her it would have tipped them off if I hadn't shown up with breakfast, and that I did this for the team. That's why I'm keeping my phone off, so she can't make contact and demand I haul ass out of here. In truth, I'm here to handle some personal business.

Yesterday, just as I was leaving the compound for what should have been my final breakfast run, I saw a delivery truck from the local computer store—if you can call eighty kilometers away local. Back in the village my team has been calling home, I followed up on a hunch and found an increase in activity coming from one of the compound's IP addresses. The user tried to mask it, hiding behind web proxies, but I'm better at his game than he is.

Pavlo isn't the only overnight arrival. He brought his hacker-for-hire with him.

If I were Marchuk, the hacker would have been fired two weeks ago, the day he left open a back door I could exploit. I was able to access Marchuk's database of arms suppliers, traders, and buyers—who they were, where they were located, what they bought—everything but who they were buying it for.

We needed to flush out the buyers, so I planted rumors about the security breach on a couple of secret forums. We also needed feet-on-the-ground intelligence about his base of operations, so we could prepare for the arrival of agents from every militant separatist group Marchuk ever armed, who were coming to take him down. But news of my breach spread so quickly, we were forced to move faster than planned. The only play we had with such little notice was to send in the least suspicious operative on our team—a high-school junior who spoke the right languages and already understood the full scope of the mission. That's how I became the compound's food runner and earned my chance to show everyone I was more than a kid with a laptop.

We came here for both Pavlo and his father, the head of the operation. The Marchuks are seriously dangerous people, but my boss considers the target *I'm* after—Pavlo's hired-gun hacker—a small-time mercenary. She shut me down when I took the information to her. Most people would have stopped there, because most people hate their jobs and their bosses. Not me. I love my job and like my boss. Underestimating this hacker will be her one regret in this whole mission, the loose thread that comes back to haunt us all one day.

I'm not going to let that happen.

I check the cheap watch I bought in the market yesterday, having anticipated not being able to use my phone. I have an hour before the raid begins, forty-five minutes more than I need. But as I approach the house, my stomach sinks a little. This is my first field mission, and right now I would trade in all my classroom training for a little real-world field experience. All of this activity around the compound—the distracted guard, the change in my schedule—maybe I'm reading it all wrong. Maybe all of this is bad. Maybe they know today's the day. *My* people will know that *they* know, which means I may not have as much time as I think. The smell of potatoes and sausage that made my mouth water a minute ago now makes my stomach turn, and I have to fight the urge to dry heave. Or run.

But it's too late for second thoughts. Marchuk Sr. is standing in the front door like he's been waiting for me, even though I changed my schedule.

"Pierre, you are here early today."

That's two more unusual things. One of the armed guards usually opens the door, and Marchuk Sr. doesn't call me Pierre. On my first delivery day, he asked my name, converted it to Ukrainian, and announced that that was what I'd be called as long as I was in his home. He looks tired. Another sinking feeling in my stomach. Was he up all night because he got word about us? The weight of the phone still in my pocket assures me a little. My lifeline.

"Sorry, sir. I found extra work planting spring barley. I start today. I hope delivering breakfast early is not too much inconvenience."

"Food deliverer, and now farmhand. A recent arrival to our village, and already you have two jobs, yes?"

"Yes, sir. We must take jobs when they are presented, since they are difficult to come by in my country."

"In Tunisia, yes? And yet your Ukrainian is near perfect."

I can't help but wonder if that's an observation or an indictment.

"Of course," Marchuk Sr. continues, "you speak your native Arabic and French, but you also speak excellent Russian."

"Russian and Ukrainian are so similar. And I have an affinity for languages, sir."

I bet he's thinking I don't resemble most of the Tunisians who have made Ukraine, with its Swiss-cheese borders, part of their migration route into the European Union. He'd be right, since I'm a black guy from Georgia—the one in the United States, not the one just 1,500 kilometers from my current location—but until now, I never worried that Marchuk Sr. knew the difference. He puts his hand on my back as I step into the house, and I stiffen before realizing it isn't an act of aggression, but the total opposite—very unlike the man. I'm still glad for the four inches of height and thirty pounds of muscle I have on him.

"I admire you, Pierre."

The morning is full of surprises for both of us, though Marchuk Sr. doesn't yet know about his. At least I hope he doesn't.

"You are an industrious young man. My layabout son takes nothing seriously, is only concerned about spending my money on women and drink. He could learn something from you."

All the curtains are drawn. As my eyes adjust to the darkness of the house, I look around the room for the lazy son, glad to find he isn't here. Pavlo Marchuk Jr. doesn't like me—or anyone else, as far as I can tell. He was only here for three days before he left, but that was all I needed to figure out he lived in a constant state of being pissed-off because his father made another man, not his only son and namesake, his second-in-command. Then, just this week, Marchuk Sr. changed his mind and gave Pavlo the job. That hasn't changed Junior's disposition one iota. Hearing his father praise even a lowly food deliverer as his better is just the kind of thing to set Pavlo off. I don't need that today. I must stay focused on finding the hacker and getting the hell out while I still can. The clock is ticking.

I want to ask him what changed his mind about making his son second-in-command, considering his low view of Pavlo, but I'm not even supposed to know, or care, about his business. Instead I say, "Thank you, sir. I will just take this to the kitchen."

I hold out the box of food, as though my reason might be different than it has been the last two weeks, but I shouldn't have. The movement draws up my sleeves, exposing my wrists, along with the watch I don't usually wear. A small thing to most, but probably not Marchuk. Before he went to the dark side, he spent twenty years in my line of work. That's about twenty years longer than I have. Experience trumps youth and size nearly every time.

"No, not in the kitchen today," he says, keeping his attention on the activity in front of the house. "They are busy in there . . . packing our things."

More like whipping up a few Molotov cocktails for the road, but I play dumb.

"You're leaving?"

"I have business abroad and must leave immediately."

"Immediately, sir?"

Marchuk looks at me for a second, and I wonder if I seem a little too eager about his departure. He reaches into his pocket, and again I prepare for the worst. And again he surprises me, pulling out a wad of money—American dollars—and handing it to me.

"Yes, you will have to find a new second job, but don't worry. It won't be difficult for a hard worker like you, Petro," he says, this time calling me by my Ukrainian name. "As soon as everything is ready, we must leave."

I bet they must, now that Junior is back and the black ops teams of several pissed-off clients are right behind him.

"I will stay out of the way in the kitchen," I say, hoping I don't sound pushy.

"No. Leave it. The men can take breakfast there, in the dining room, if they want. They are too busy, anyway."

I put the box of food where he directs me to, but this isn't good. I need access to the kitchen. Marchuk's office is on the other side of it, and I'm certain that's where the hacker is. Marchuk is standing in the door, just as he was when I arrived, as though he's still expecting someone who clearly isn't the food runner. He's distracted, but not so much that I can sneak into the kitchen without him noticing. I begin taking the food out of the box and placing it on the coffee table, but accidentally-on-purpose drop a large container of dumpling soup.

"Oh no, the rug! I will get a towel," I say, running for the kitchen before Marchuk Sr. can stop me.

I make it to the swinging kitchen door, surprised he hasn't followed. I'm even more surprised to find no one there. No bomb-making materials on the table, either. Just free-and-clear access to the office. But when I reach it, I'm disappointed to find the office doesn't yield any clues, either. In fact, the room is completely empty. It has been stripped bare of computers, file cabinets, desks, everything. Not a single sticky note on the wall over the place where the computer monitor used to be. No impression left behind on a notepad that I could run a pencil over to reveal a clue. The hacker is gone.

Coming to the compound might have risked our operation—I'm definitely risking my life—and all for nothing.

But I don't have time to feel fear or regret. Only thing left for me to do is get the hell out of here before it's too late. As I pass through the kitchen, I grab a towel so I can at least make a show of cleaning up the soup.

I push open the swinging door at the very moment Marchuk Sr. yells out, "They are here!"

It takes my brain a second to wonder if "they" are friend or foe, and then another second to realize it doesn't really matter. Marchuk has drawn his sidearm and pointed it into the yard, but my entry must throw him, because he turns to look at me.

"Petro, get down!"

Another second passes and the house is under attack, the staccato of AR-15 gunfire outside drowning out every sound except for the pinging of ammo ricocheting off every surface inside. Marchuk Sr. is now on the floor three feet inside the house, knocked that far back by the shot that has to have killed him instantly. I dive behind the concrete wall that separates the living and dining areas and speed-dial my boss. I can hear a volley of gunfire outside, most likely between the men loading the truck and whoever "they" are, but I suspect one of the Marchuk family's clients has arrived before my team began our own incursion.

"The Marchuk compound is under fire," I say the moment I hear her voice on the other end. "I don't know who it is but—"

"Peter, where the hell are you?"

I'm afraid to tell her, but I'm also afraid of dying today, and the bullets have not stopped flying. "At the compound, in the dining room. I know I shouldn't be, but I couldn't leave without—hold on. They stopped firing for some reason."

"The reason is because that's *us* out there. Marchuk's people began moving out early. We had to stop him. He drew on us first." She's silent for a minute before she adds, "After all our work, I could kill you for ruining this operation, Peter."

"You almost did, boss." It's a smartass thing to say, but that's my defense mechanism when I'm in trouble, and I am currently in some serious shit.

Now, in the silence that almost seems as deafening as the shooting that came before it, I hear the crunching of boots on bits of pulverized concrete. I jam the phone into my pocket, leaving it on, and search the room for a weapon. There isn't one, which is ironic considering the family's line of work. Not that I could reach it in time anyway.

Even before I see him, I can smell him from the other side of the wall: B.O. mixed with beets, onions, and pickled cabbage. Since I arrived, I've come to love the scent of borscht, but not when it oozes secondhand from Marchuk Jr.'s already-rank pores. He doesn't know I'm here, so even if he's armed, I may be able to take him.

Or maybe not. My head is spinning and I have to lean against the wall just to keep my balance.

"I saw an old car parked outside the gate. I don't recognize it."

And I don't recognize that voice, which means Pavlo is not alone. No way can I take on two armed men, especially since I'm currently sliding down the wall into a sitting position, as though my body has a will of its own. I'm losing feeling in my right leg. What the hell is happening to me?

"I saw it arrive each morning before I left for Kiev. Belongs to the delivery boy. He must still be here," Pavlo says.

"They stopped shooting for some reason. We should go while we can. They have our vehicles surrounded. We can go out back, make an end around, maybe reach the boy's car."

"Father liked him. That may be why he drew his weapon and then hesitated in firing—because he was worried about the boy. It is his fault my father is dead."

Pavlo is right. I was the last thing his father ever saw. I startled him, but I still think he would have taken the shot at my team, whether I'd come through the kitchen door at just that moment or not. But I won't ever forget the way he looked at me in that moment. He knew I'd be the last thing he'd ever see. Even if he was a very bad guy, I won't ever forget that.

"Then find him, kill him, and let's go."

"Kill him?" Pavlo says, sounding incredulous. Yeah, I'm with Pavlo.

Thank God my boss knows I'm in here. I just need to stay alive long enough for the team to get me.

"I thought you want revenge?"

"This is why Father would not want you in charge, Koval. As the Americans say, you are a one-trick pony. A gun is your answer to everything."

"If a gun was not the answer to everything, you would not be a wealthy man."

"We find the boy, use him as a hostage, as a human shield, to get out," Pavlo explains. "*Then* we kill him."

Oh no. He's made me. He knows who I am and who just invaded his compound and killed his dad, and now he's going to . . . wait, what was I just saying? I feel so light-headed.

"There is no army in the world that would sacrifice killing you to save a simple delivery boy. I was a rebel soldier before I could drive a car. No one cared that I was a boy," says the other guy, making his case too convincingly for my comfort, but at least they have no idea who I am. "They will kill him, then you. You will die like your father. Forget the boy. We should go while we still can."

They'll have to come around the wall and pass through the dining room to reach the back of the house, the escape route they're planning to take to get outside the compound to my car. Their boots crunch on concrete as they come closer.

I want to run, but every bit of strength has drained from me. All I can do is play dead.

But I won't have to play. Marchuk comes around the wall and, despite what he just told the other guy, draws his gun the second our eyes meet.

Next thing I know, the whole world goes black.

When I wake up, I expect to be tied up in an abandoned farmhouse in the wilds of Ukraine, so I'm surprised to find myself in a hospital bed. We must be near the Luhansk front line because the building is shaking as though the area is under heavy artillery fire. I try to focus on the things closest to the bed: a vitals-monitoring machine, a bag of saline slowly dripping into a vein in my arm. Everything is written in English. Everything is modern and shiny. I look over at the dim left side of the room, and make out a person sitting in the chair two feet away. Instinctively I search for a weapon, but then a voice comes from the dark. I recognize it immediately.

"You're alive, then. Are you more than that?"

I am now, thanks to the burst of sunlight I'm assaulted with as she slides open a window at the foot of my bed. Weird place for a window. Oh, wait. I'm slowly getting it. That isn't heavy artillery shaking the building, but heavy turbulence. I'm not in a hospital. I'm in a jet. I look past the woman and see two more patients in hospital beds. I don't know who they are, but they must be in worse shape than I am because they're hooked up to way more machines.

"Do you know who I am?"

When I first saw her in the dim light, I thought she was my mother. They look something alike. Similar coloring, anyway. But a few more seconds of consciousness reminds me how impossible that is.

"Of course. Who are *they*?" I ask, pointing at my fellow patients.

"The men who saved your life."

"Saved my life? Last thing I remember—"

"You lost a lot of blood, but the doctor says you'll be fine."

"I was shot?"

"You took shrapnel. A piece of concrete pierced your femoral artery, but you're in much better shape than they are."

I don't remember feeling the pain of the concrete hitting me, but that explains why I felt so weak. I must have passed out from the blood loss. But I don't remember anything after that.

"What happened? Did we get Pavlo?"

Rogers doesn't answer right away. I watch as her expression goes from sad to worried, before it lands on angry.

"Once I knew you were inside the compound, our job became an extraction mission. So no, we didn't get him."

"But you should have—"

"Sacrificed you for the mission? Can you imagine the hell I'd have caught back home once they found out I let a sixteen-year-old work such a dangerous mission?"

We both know that no one ever finds out about most of what we do—that's the whole point of what we do—but I don't question her. Considering the status of the two men lying in the other beds, I ask an even stupider question.

"Is my cover blown?"

She stares at me for a moment too long, like she's trying to decide whether to do more damage to me than the shrapnel already has.

"I mean, I think I remember Marchuk seeing me. He could probably identify me, and—"

"Your cover may be the only thing to come out of this mission in one piece. I'm sure Pavlo still thinks you're a food runner from the village, if he thinks of you at all." I want to stop her, to tell her he blames me for his father's death, so yeah, he probably thinks of me. But I stay quiet and let Rogers continue. "He probably has other things on his mind. We aren't the only ones looking for him."

"And the other one?"

"What other one?" she asks, leaning forward, gripping the arms of her chair.

"Pavlo was with someone else, someone new whose voice I didn't recognize. He was Ukrainian, though. His dialect was eastern, same as the Marchuks, and he had a Ukrainian name, though I don't remember it right now."

My boss smiles. This is something she didn't know before. I can tell she's already drafting the memo in her head about there being a second man to escape the compound.

It probably isn't much, since I don't know his name—though the way she's smiling suggests she knows who I'm talking about—but it's more intel than she had before I regained consciousness. That's huge in a business that is all about the exchange of information. She gives me something in return.

"We found you in the corner of the room against the wall. You were in the fetal position, your face hidden, lying in about two pints of your own blood. You'd gone into shock." Rogers hesitates when she says this, and for just a moment, I think maybe she actually feels something about that. About me being hurt. But then she goes back to being just my boss. "If they even saw you, I'm sure they left you for dead. Don't worry about your cover."

Those words make me feel better than whatever painkillers they're pumping into me. It means I can go back into the field as soon as my leg has healed up. It means I can keep the only job I've ever wanted, even if I didn't really know I wanted it until the moment Marchuk pulled his weapon on me and I thought I'd lost the job, much less everything else.

"Oh man, that's great news, because—"

Rogers raises her hand to stop me. "Peter, given this conversation we just had, I assume you are lucid and comprehend what I'm saying?"

"Sure, boss."

"Good, because I'd hate to say this to you if you weren't at full mental capacity, lest you misunderstand."

"Misunderstand?"

She leaves her chair, comes over to stand at my bedside, and looks down at me. Wow. She looks pissed. I know what she's about to say. I'm under reprimand, I'm headed back to my computer and desk where I belong, she never should have approved me for fieldwork, I'll be—

"You're fired, Peter."

CHAPTER 1

Colorado, U.S.A. | Fall Semester

It's just after twenty-one hundred hours, and the track and field complex is deserted, but I can't shake the feeling I'm being followed. Seven months after leaving Ukraine, I'm still not convinced people aren't after me, but tonight my paranoia feels less irrational. Someone's out there.

Everyone else at Carlisle Academy should be in the dorms cramming for this week's midterms, but I'm not alone. The night is pitch black and I can't see a thing beyond the few lights around the track, so I rely on my other senses. Still running—in case flight is a better option than fight—I tune out the drone of crickets and hear someone moving along the boxwood hedge lining the port side of the track, twenty feet away. Beneath the scent of piñon pines in the hills above campus, I detect the pungent aroma of pizza from Buy-the-Slice. Which is in town, four point three miles from campus.

I stop running and turn toward the hedge, beyond relieved that there isn't a Ukrainian arms dealer lying in wait behind them.

"Bunker, get out here."

No one responds but the crickets.

"Bunk, I know it's you. No one in his right mind would put garlic, gorgonzola, anchovies, and kimchi on a pizza."

Sure enough, Bunker emerges from behind the bushes, a half-eaten slice in hand. For a guy who's only five-foot-four, the man can eat. He's *always* eating. But it's understandable. He has a lot of making up to do in the food department. Well, pretty much the whole life-experiences department.

"See," Bunk says around a mouthful of pizza, "that's why I can never seem to get the jump on you no matter how stealthy I am."

"Hate to break it to you, but you're not all that stealthy," I tell him. "Why are you here, anyway?"

"I was at the library and thought you might want a ride home. And don't try to change the subject. There is no way you should have smelled this food from that far away," Bunker says, stuffing the last of the pizza into his mouth. "Either you're a dog-boy or a highly trained killing machine or a covert operative, but you are *not* a mere mortal."

I try not to let Bunker's accusations rattle me, and resume my run, hoping the fact that he is the most out-of-shape sixteen-year-old I've ever met will keep him from joining me. Until last year, he spent his entire life living in a bunker, hence his nickname. His dad took baby Bunk underground on New Year's Eve 1999 and waited for the end of the world for everyone without his foresight and provision-hoarding skills. He didn't want to give space to any gym equipment besides a full set of barbells, convinced jogging in place would be enough. It wasn't. Bunker's built like a five-foot-four Mr. Olympia but has the stamina of a toddler.

But he won't let a lack of oxygen get in the way of continuing his weeklong interrogation. Bunker has been hitting me nonstop with theories about my "true identity" ever since he witnessed me kick the asses of five townies in the alley behind Buy-the-Slice. It was a regrettable display of force—especially for the townies—but necessary. I've sworn him to silence about the whole thing, and he's been true to his word, except when it comes to me.

Despite the whole Joe Cool thing I've managed to pull off so far, the truth is, his questions are stressing me out way more than any I'll find on a midterm exam. I barely made it out of Ukraine with my cover intact after managing to dupe Marchuk Sr. for weeks. I'd hate to have it blown by a guy who learned everything he knows about interrogation from old cop shows.

"So . . . I'm still not buying that story about your dad teaching you a few defensive moves," Bunker says, already starting to pant a little. "Taking out five Crestview High football players with only a six-pack of soda for a weapon is not like fending off a mugger in the mall parking lot."

"You helped. Some."

"By the time I figured out what the hell was going on, you'd already knocked three of them unconscious."

It's October, but unseasonably warm for Colorado. I stop running for a second, peel off my sweat-drenched t-shirt, and search for a dry inch I can use to wipe my glasses, but I only make them worse. I drop the shirt on the ground next to the track and place the glasses on top of it, noticing my hands are shaking just a bit. If Bunker and his questions are making me nervous, I hate to think what kind of mess I'd be if there *had* been an arms-dealing terrorist behind the hedge.

"Take, for example, those specs," Bunker says. "You think you're pulling a Clark Kent, but you're fooling no one."

"I'm pulling a what?"

"Superman's flimsy disguise? Lois Lane might be hotter, but I'm a lot more observant. There is zero prescription in those lenses."

"Way hotter," I say, hoping to get his focus off me and onto his favorite subject. When you grow up with only your dad for company, you miss out on a lot. Bunker lost about four years of lusting over real live girls that he will never make up for.

Unfortunately, he doesn't take the bait.

"Despite the glasses, playing clarinet in the band, that sermon you gave me last weekend about the difference between hacking code and code-hacking, even your mad D&D skills, you are not a geek," he says, shaking long red curls out of his face. They immediately flop back over his forehead, nearly covering his eyes, like a sheepdog's. "In fact, your whole cover is a cliché. *Nobody* is that much of a nerd, even the hipsters trying hard to be nerds because it's cool now, and I should know. Besides, real geeks don't usually have biceps like that."

"Um," I say, as I point to him and back to me again. He might need one of those spray-on tans, since Bunker's the whitest white boy I know—due to his only source of ultraviolet light since birth being a battery-operated lamp, and just enough to prevent rickets—but he would blow me away in a bodybuilding contest.

"Yeah, but I'm a freak thanks to fifteen years under-ground with nothing to entertain me but weights and my dad's pre-millennium comic book and DVD collection. I'm The Thing from Fantastic Four. You, my friend, look like a boy-bander with a well-used gym membership. *Big* dif-ference. A guy who looks like you cannot be oblivious that he looks like you."

Speaking of looks, I give one to Bunker that suggests he's given way too much thought about mine.

"What?" Bunker asks, looking genuinely surprised by my reaction. "I'm just trying to make the point that you are fooling no one."

Actually, I'd been fooling everyone, including Bunker, until the Buy-the-Slice alley incident. That was the exact opposite of flying under the radar and a total rookie mis-take. But I go into denial mode anyway. You *always* deny.

"I think you inherited your father's gift of paranoia, Bunk. Sorry, but no one can live underground for one-point-five decades and not be a little . . ." I finish the sentence by twirling my index finger next to my head.

"See, that's what I mean. A regular person would just say fifteen years, or maybe one and a half decades, not 'one-point-five.' The way you talk sometimes is so, I don't know, *precise*. And you know all those languages."

"This is Carlisle. Plenty of people here speak multiple languages."

"You speak *five*. I'm pretty sure there has never been another student in the whole history of Carlisle, one alleg-edly born in the United States, who spoke Farsi, Urdu, *and* Mandarin," Bunker says, making me wish I'd never divulged my aptitude with foreign languages. Good thing I never told him I actually speak eight. Nine if you include the Tlingit I picked up working a summer job in Alaska, but I'm not really fluent in that, so it probably doesn't count.

"I mean, when the most pedestrian foreign language you speak is Ukrainian—"

"Stop," I say, and not only because Bunker's now wheezing like an old man, or because the word *Ukraine* is like my Kryptonite. It's mostly because I know we're not alone. The *shhh* sound I just heard didn't come from either of us.

Bunker bends over, hands on knees, obviously grateful for the break. For the second time tonight, I tune out the crickets, and now Bunker's raspy wheezing, and listen. The intruder has gone silent, but I know he's there. It could be another student come to burn off some midterm stress with a late run. Or it could be an assassin dispatched by Pavlo Marchuk. There has been no sign of him since he escaped our capture, and word is one of his clients found him before we could, which would make him very dead if true. But that doesn't mean he didn't take out a contract on me before he kicked off, intent on avenging his father from beyond the grave.

Okay, now I'm the one being paranoid. They can't possibly know I'm here, or who I am. Still . . . someone is out there, watching me.

I take a defensive stance—imperceptible, at least, to anyone but Bunker—who has regained the ability to breathe.

"What is it?" he asks, looking around us. "Is someone after you?"

I ignore his questions and scan the field beyond the track, looking for points of entry I may have missed.

"Look, Bunk," I whisper, "if something goes down in

the next minute, don't try to play tough like you did in the alley last week. Just run like hell and get help."

Bunk looks simultaneously terrified and vindicated. "I knew you weren't just mild-mannered Peter Smith. *Smith*. Is that even your real—"

I put my finger to my lips. Still I hear nothing. But the wind stirs, and I detect a familiar scent in the direction of the same hedge Bunker hid behind. Floral, but in a chemical way. Perfume. Girls.

No sooner do I think it than a gang of them jumps from behind the boxwoods, their leader pointing a weapon that I fear almost as much as Japanese shurikens (*hate* those): her phone.

All I can make out of her is shiny blond hair and long red nails wrapped around the phone as it creates a momentary flash of light.

Five townies seeking revenge, even Ukrainian black ops, I'm prepared to handle. But giggling, camera-wielding girls? What are they doing out here in the dark, anyway—stalking me just to get a picture? I'm not *that* good-looking, no matter what Bunker says.

I'm thrown off my guard for a few seconds. By the time I regain it, the damage is done. They've taken my photo and are already running away toward the dorms, their laughter sounding conspiratorial. They might as well have hurled a ninja star at my heart.

CHAPTER 2

By morning, I've put the camera incident into better perspective. It was weird and random, but equating a bunch of freshmen taking my photo to a ninja-star attack was a total overreaction. Bunker said it only confirmed his point about me looking like a member of a boy band, suggesting they just wanted a photo of me with my shirt off. He also was convinced the girls had put me and my cover in grave danger, though I had neither confirmed nor denied the fact that I even have a cover.

The thing is, Bunker is mostly right. I technically do still work for the Company, also known as the CIA. Rogers's high-school recruitment program, Operation Early Bird, will likely be shut down, but I was able to talk her out of completely firing me and agreed to an indefinite suspension. I also convinced her to get me enrolled at Carlisle Academy. I told her I chose Carlisle and its stellar STEM programs for my senior year because it was always a dream of mine to attend. I also pointed out that, given the student body, I could amass quality intel on some of the nation's top science research laboratories and the scientists working inside them. The Company is never supposed to spy on the homeland, and technically I'm off the job, so it was a hard offer to refuse.

Rogers wrote in the Ukraine final incident report that I was good at what I did, but tended to get a little too "emotionally invested." Until Rogers recruited me, I hadn't been emotionally invested in anything. I was only hacking because I could, because no one could stop me, because it was all I had of my own. This job gave me a reason to . . . I don't know, just *a reason,* period. So hell yeah, I get worked up about it sometimes. Rogers doesn't see it that way, but I'll prove her wrong when my skills *and* my passion for my job help me capture the most dangerous member of Marchuk's team. Pavlo may be dead, but I've been watching his hacker-for-hire since we left Ukraine. Over the summer, I caught him monitoring our defense command center down in Colorado Springs, as well as some of our country's top research labs right here in town, and in my book that makes him a threat to national security. Which is why I've tracked him to Carlisle.

Even before Rogers gave me the job, I always kept a low profile because of being, well, a criminal. I was never a fan of selfies or social media, so it wasn't hard to stay low. But once I started hacking for the right side of the law and became an operative, the Company searched for and removed every trace of me or my face from the internet. What they say about the internet being forever? It's true unless the CIA eradicates the old you and creates the fake you.

So while I got zero sleep thinking about the girl with

the camera, remembering my bigger mission has kept me from freaking out. At least until Bunker found me at my locker this morning.

"Bro, how're you holding up?" he asks me. "I'm guessing not well, since you sneaked out of the house so early this morning."

Bunker's just worried about me, but I can't deal with an interrogation this morning, so I fake being chill about the whole thing.

"I didn't sneak . . . I just wanted to get my mind right for the calculus exam today and used the walk to think," I say, banging on my stuck locker door until it finally unsticks and flies open. "Wouldn't happen to have any WD-40 on you, would you?"

But Bunker will not be distracted.

"You had the Morrisons worried, but I covered for you," Bunker says, referring to our host family. He was assigned to them because he's attending Carlisle on a scholarship that doesn't include the outrageous boarding fees. I live there because spies who are suspended, and gathering intel that is only potentially useful, rate the lowest expense budgets possible. "Mrs. Morrison made me bring you this."

He hands me a brown paper bag. I open it to find a partially eaten blueberry muffin, half a banana, and a string cheese wrapper, and give it back along with some serious side-eye.

"I got hungry on the drive to school," he says, looking guilty as he stuffs it into his *Phantom Menace* backpack, a relic from his dad's bunker. I tried to tell him no one beyond middle school carries a Star Wars backpack, and certainly not one from a movie two decades old, but Bunker doesn't care about that kind of thing. He likes what he likes, including my food, apparently.

Just thinking about that muffin makes my stomach growl, but missing breakfast was worth avoiding another interrogation from Bunker. Of course, he'd have tried to mask his questions, but Bunk isn't exactly a whiz at subterfuge. It's hard to learn the nuances of interpersonal deception—also known as lying—when you spend your whole life with only one person, sharing a three-hundred-square-foot space. Pretty hard to hide anything in that situation.

"Look, we've only known each other a short time, but we're already like brothers from another mother. Except for you actually *being* a brother. Wait—since I'm not black, is it okay for me to call you that?" Bunker asks, but doesn't wait for an answer. "What I'm saying is, you can confide in me. Come on, aren't you just a little worried about . . . *the incident*?"

I consider pretending I have no idea what he's talking about, but I know evasion won't work with Bunker. He'll only pester me until I concede or punch him in the face. I like Bunk; in fact, he's my only friend at Carlisle, even if we aren't quite at the 'brother' level yet. That's something Rogers would consider further evidence of my emotional attachment issues. An operative should never have actual friends, only assets.

Still, I'd rather avoid punching Bunker in the face, so I try a confusion tactic instead.

"I'll admit I had a hard time getting to sleep last night. Depending on how those freshmen frame the whole thing, if she ever saw that photo, Darlene would make my life hell."

"Darlene?"

"My girlfriend, you know, back home in Texas? I told you about her."

"No, sir, you did not. First time I have ever heard of this Darlene person," Bunker says, sounding skeptical. I don't dare look at his face to get a read. Not that I need to. It's clear from his voice he doesn't believe me. "How is it possible that we've shared a home for eight weeks and I have never heard a single mention of a girlfriend 'back home'?"

"Because when I left, things weren't so great between us. She was angry I'd chosen Carlisle over her. I wasn't sure there was anything to tell," I explain, feigning interest in something buried deep inside my locker. "But we've been talking and, you know, working it out with the long-distance thing. So yeah, I'm a little worried about what they might do with the picture."

I peek around my locker door and manage an expression of worry that must convince Bunker, because he seems to buy the story.

"And what about *her*?" Bunker says in a low voice. "Is *you-know-who* aware of Darlene?"

He nods to someone across the hall, but I don't turn around to see who's there.

I already know.

"She wouldn't care," I say, crushed as I am to admit it.

"I get it," Bunker says, nodding knowingly. "You haven't told her."

"There's nothing between us, so there's no reason to

tell," I say, hoping Bunker senses I might actually punch him in the face.

"Uh huh, that's why you couldn't stop talking about her after you guys went out that one time. Didn't sound like 'nothing' to me."

"Like you said, it was a one-time thing, okay? Moving on." This time, my tone should make it clear even to Bunker that the Q&A session is over.

He stares at me for a second, and while I'm a good actor—nature of the job and all—I get the feeling Bunker hasn't believed a word I've said since he walked up. I see in his expression that he's forming another question, but he must think better of it.

"You probably haven't been online this morning, given your aversion to the internet," Bunker says, and then it's like I can see the cartoon light bulb go on over his head. "Which *could* point to you actually being Peter Smith, mild-mannered prep-school student, because a *you-know-what* would be on the dark web infiltrating sleeper cells and black-hat networks—"

"I think you mean the *deep* web—not the same thing."

"—on the other hand, your aversion to social media is the appropriate response of someone flying under the radar," Bunker says, ignoring my correction. "Anyway, I already know how those girls will frame it."

I get this sinking feeling, like when the teacher is handing out graded exams and you're pretty sure you bombed.

"What are you talking about?"

"You really need to get online more often. For all your talk about hacking code, or code-hacking, or whatever—"

I stop him before he can go off on another tangent. "What were you saying about the freshmen?"

"Oh, right," Bunker says, handing me his phone. "I'd look like a sweaty mess in desperate need of a shower. Thanks to the born-with-it tan and six-pack abs, you manage to look like a glistening Adonis."

I take the phone and give Bunker a look that says, *Stop saying crap like that.*

There's the photo on Twitter—my expression looking like someone just told me I won the Powerball instead of the fear and anger I felt at the time—along with a caption: *See Prettyboy run.* My stomach drops, but only for a second, before my brain pushes that reflexive feeling away. They posted it last night to the account @*CarlisleAcademy,* and so far, it has been retweeted a couple hundred times.

Wow. That's kind of a lot, but I pretend like I'm not worried about it. The hacker has no idea I'm on his tail, and no idea what I look like. He was only at the compound for a few hours before my team's incursion and, on the off chance he saw me, it had to have been from a distance. I look a helluva lot different than I did then, and not just from the addition of eyeglasses. Here, I'm clean-shaven and let my hair grow out into a high fade. In Ukraine, my hair was barely there and I had ditched my razor for a few weeks.

"You and a few of her closest friends are the only ones who even care," I say, returning his phone. "Stop worrying. It ain't nothing but a thing."

And it really isn't, when I consider why I'm even at Carlisle. I was there when Rogers vouched for me, saying I had the makings of a great operative. I may be on suspension, tasked with an assignment-not-really, and everyone in the office probably thinks Early Bird is a horrible idea after my Ukraine performance, but I see it as my shot at redemption, and I don't plan to screw it up.

CHAPTER 3

After the first-period bell rings, I put the photo out of my mind and replace it with the other thing that has kept me up worrying more than a few nights, which isn't hard to do since she sits two rows in front of me.

Katie Carmichael is the "her" Bunker thinks might want to know about the nonexistent Darlene. But he couldn't be more wrong. I could spontaneously combust right here in front of Mr. Maitland's World Geo class, and she wouldn't bother to throw the contents of her water bottle on me.

As I walk down the row to my desk, I pretend I don't even see Katie. But I must fail miserably. She makes a point of turning to ask a question of the girl next to her, going out of her way to be oblivious to me.

Bunker notices it too, and whispers, "Oooh, it's chilly in here. Guess you were right," as we take our seats beside each other.

Maybe I should back up a minute, because I've probably presented Katie in a poor light when she isn't the bad guy in our failed equation. That's totally on me. I was initially focused on her because I thought she was the hacker I'm after. She was new to Carlisle, like Bunker and me, which automatically put her on my list. I'd been tracking my target through his signature, which is how some hackers mark their work. Sort of the way taggers tag their graffiti. It seems counterintuitive for a hacker to leave clues, especially one who has been trying—unsuccessfully, thanks to yours truly—to infiltrate our national security agencies, but some are so impressed with their own skills, they taunt hacker-trackers like me into trying to catch them. Sounds stupid, but these guys are actually geniuses. The type who tag their work are also classic narcissists. Aka assholes on crack.

Katie is not that, despite the whole wouldn't-put-me-out-if-I-was-on-fire thing. Not that I can blame her. In eight short weeks, she's become Carlisle's star soccer player. She's already poised to take the crown away from whoever won last year's Most Popular Girl Ever. And the engineering club overthrew their three-term president in favor of Katie Carmichael as their leader. But don't cry for the deposed ex-president. He took her to homecoming. That's Katie's problem, and mine: her unassailable likability. And the fact that she's drop-dead hot. Plus, she's got that English accent. Even the way she pronounces my name, *Pee-tah,* makes me—

"Mr. Smith, did you hear me, or is communication with you an exercise in futility this morning? Hello—is anyone home?"

I'm so focused on staring at the back of Katie's head that Maitland startles me nearly out of my seat, appearing out of nowhere and rapping his knuckles on my desk.

"Um . . . I . . . uh . . . I mean, what was the question, sir?"

"Brilliant. Scintillating. But don't overexert yourself for

our sakes," Maitland says, being his usual special self. The guy hates me for reasons unknown.

"Sorry, I'm a little sleepy this morning. Stayed up too late last night watching *Seabiscuit*. Ever seen that movie, Mr. Maitland?"

He gives me the evil eye but doesn't say another word about my lack of brilliance. Oh, riiight, that's the reason he hates me. A while back, I arrived at his class early, hoping to corner Katie into having more than a one-word conversation, but caught Maitland on the phone making book on a horse. He tried to play it off, but I knew his game. Before I discovered the money I could make from hacking, one of my hustles was hunting unclaimed betting tickets.

I'd take a Greyhound from Atlanta to the Birmingham dog track, sneak inside, and spend the whole weekend picking tickets off the ground, left there by people who didn't have time to stand in line to cash out a five- or ten-dollar ticket. Cash in enough of them, though? Even after I'd pay out my partner—I've always been a decent con artist, but no teller is going to cash tickets for a twelve-year-old—I'd clear two or three hundred dollars and get back home before the truancy officer could report me to Children's Services. It was easy enough as long as I had a half-assed foster family—and I had a few—who looked the other way if I spent a night or two away from home, so long as they got their tiny government check.

So, I know a pick-six from a superfecta. Both are pretty desperate bets, and I overheard Maitland place big money on both. I called him on it, and he called it the "sport of kings," like giving it a snob name could cover the fact that he was violating Carlisle's code of ethics. Yeah, I see you,

Maitland. And he knows it, which is why he moves on to other prey.

"Ms. Carmichael, perhaps you can enlighten us?"

When Katie looks back at me, I detect a fleeting glimmer of sympathy. Or maybe not, since the eye-roll she gives me is not quite as fleeting. That I read clearly. Then she dismisses me with a toss of that dark, shiny hair I remember smelled so good and made me think of strawberries and vanilla cream. Even her hair smells English.

"Charlemagne's march across Europe and his subsequent formation of the Carolingian Empire was driven by his desire to spread Christianity," she says. "But his success in conquering the Saxons pointed to the possibility that he was motivated by territorial aggrandizement as much as religious fervor."

For three seconds, the whole room is quiet—even Maitland, who is never at a loss for words. Intelligence delivered in that accent? Katie Carmichael can make even "territorial aggrandizement" sound good. I mean, she's perfect, in a good way. I just can't believe she could be the one who tried to crack NORAD a few months ago. Plus, when you look like her—olive skin that kinda seems to glow, brown eyes with flecks of something else in them, and her lips—well, why waste all that sitting in a room behind a computer? The bad guys would have to be idiots not to put an operative like that to better use in the field, no matter how mad her cracking skills are. That's one reason why I ruled her out as the hacker. She's brilliant, gorgeous, and the complete opposite of an asshole. Everyone loves Katie, including Maitland, and the only other thing he seems to love is hearing himself speak.

I had to end things the morning after our first real date—dinner and a movie in town, followed by half an hour in the back seat of her car making out. There's another thing she could win awards for. She's *the* best kisser.

Of course I wanted more. What guy doesn't want more? But with Katie, just the kissing was enough to let me know she'd be the kind of distraction I couldn't risk. My target could be sitting right next to me decoding the Pentagon's cipher algorithms, but if Katie walked into the room, I'd probably be like, *Whatever, dude. Go for it.* So yeah, I dropped the it's-me-not-you bomb on her the next morning, which also happened to be the day before *I* was supposed to take her to homecoming.

So you can understand why she hates me.

". . . he not only shaped the new Holy Roman Empire," Katie is saying as she wraps up her answer, "but continued to influence French monarchs a thousand years after his death, as we'll see next semester when studying Bonaparte and the rise of the Napoleonic Empire."

While we're all absorbing the English-accented knowledge that has just been dropped on us, a screeching fire alarm breaks us all from our Katie Carmichael trance.

My fear instinct kicks in, but it subsides when I remind myself that this is probably a surprise drill or a prank. As we've all been instructed since kindergarten, no matter which school we attended, we keep calm and walk in single file out of the classroom and into the hall. The building is shaped like a U, and at the end of each arm is a stairwell and exit leading to the parking lot. We all follow the escape route we practiced at the beginning of the school year and head for the stairwell at the end of the corridor.

"I thought we only do one of these a semester," I say to Bunker. "Not that I'm complaining about getting out of Maitland's class for a few minutes."

"Or away from that icy indifference Katie is throwing your direction," Bunker says as he lines up behind me. "How much you wanna bet someone pulled the alarm?"

"That's a sucker bet," I say, because these things are never an actual fire, but I still keep an eye out for Katie, indifference and all, just in case for the first time in the history of ever, there's a real emergency. She's four people ahead of me, but since I have half a foot on her and a couple inches on the next tallest guy in the room, I can spot her no problem. At least, until I can't. Somewhere between the hallway and the stairwell, I lose sight of her.

What the hell? I only turned my back for a second, and now she's gone. How does a whole girl just disappear?

"Bunker, do you see Katie up ahead?"

"Are you trying to remind me I'm the shortest guy in class, or what?"

"No, it's just weird that I can't see her," I say as we pass through the rear exit doors and into the parking lot behind the school.

"Thought you didn't care for that girl. You were really insistent about it twenty minutes ago."

"I don't care who she's dating or whether she stays pissed with me forever, but I do care if she dies in a fiery inferno."

"First off, did you detect even a whiff of smoke with that canine-like olfactory system of yours? Second, remain calm. It never helps to panic. There's a reason the flight attendants always say that in airplane disaster movies."

Bunker really needs to catch up on film from the last couple of decades, but I appreciate his advice. He could not be more on point. Still, where the hell is Katie?

"Now can you spot her?"

"If you can't see her, how do you expect I can?"

Bunk's right, it *is* a desperate question. But I'm beginning to feel a little desperate. I consider breaking formation, abandoning my class's line and going back into the building, when I notice I'm being watched.

A few girls in the lines on either side of ours—one line from a freshman class, the other full of seniors—are staring at me. The freshmen are trying to hide the fact that they're staring; the older girls aren't trying to hide anything. A few of them smile, one winks suggestively, and . . . okay, that blonde at the back of the freshman line just mouthed something at me that makes me wish I didn't read lips. Almost.

Like a car wreck you know you shouldn't watch, I'm fixated on what the blond girl is suggesting we do after school, until Headmistress Dodson's voice booms through a megaphone, snapping me out of it.

That's when I realize who the blonde is—the girl who took my photo last night.

That's also when I see the top of Katie's head in the line, four people ahead of me, as though she'd never been missing.

CHAPTER 4

It turns out Bunker was right. Someone pulled an alarm and now Dodson is launching a full-scale investigation to find the culprit, which she just announced over the PA system in her usual I'm-not-screwing-around Voice-of-God way.

I'm in the cafeteria at lunch, trying to focus on my own investigation and ignore the growing number of stares I'm getting from Carlisle's female population. Since that first-period fire drill, whispering and pointing have been added to the staring. As long as I don't run into the slightly scary blond girl who must be the most aggressive freshman ever, I won't worry too much about it. I'm peeved she started all this by tweeting my picture, but I can deal as long as she keeps it at the harmless crush level. After two months on campus, my suspect list is still a couple of suspects too long to get sidetracked by crazy-making women, Katie Carmichael included.

With Marchuk dead, the hacking mercenary may now be working for someone even more dangerous, though I'm still not sure why he chose Carlisle to hide out. My best guess is because it's only ten miles from Boulder, home to several federal science agencies, one of which is working on quantum encryption technology to generate unbreakable codes to secure the nation's defense systems. A lot of the lab's scientists send their kids to Carlisle, and I'm thinking that's how the hacker plans to get close to the facility—by making friends with some of those students, worming his way into their lives, and finally gaining the access I've been shutting down with his every attempt.

Not everything is hackable; sometimes real-life people have to make real-life incursions. For a hacker who has spent months trying to breach our security systems, breaking into the National Institute of Standards and Technology would be like reaching Epic tier in Dungeons and Dragons. All that encryption technology. All those lasers. So far, I've managed to rule out three people: Katie, Bunker, and Joel Easter. They, like everyone else on my list, were presumed guilty until proven innocent because they were new enrollees this year. Fortunately, that list is small—five suspects in all—because Carlisle rarely admits new students who aren't part of the incoming freshman class, and I know my target isn't a ninth grader. He could be a child genius, but the confidence, or arrogance, it takes to tag his work suggests he's older.

Obviously, he could be a she—Katie made the list, after all—but the profile I created for the hacker says it's a guy, so I call him a he, but I keep an open mind. Joel is a level-three legacy student, which means two generations of Easters before him attended Carlisle. So he was genetically destined to attend. He didn't start until his junior year because his parents had lived in Europe until recently. Now that his family has returned stateside, he's cashing in on his Carlisle legacy. Joel's a nice guy, but I didn't take him at his word on his backstory. I had my cubicle neighbor back at Langley look into it, and his story checks out. His father is one of the top laser scientists at NIST, which puts Joel in the potential asset category.

Clearing Bunker was easier. Thanks to his previous life as a troglodyte, he didn't even know what the internet was until recently. Of course, his father knew all about it, but thought it was some kind of mind-control experiment funded by the government. Bunk's backstory was confirmed by a *Time* magazine investigative report, as well as thorough psych evals conducted by *The Journal of Applied Behavioral Research*. Yeah, Bunker and his crazy dad are kinda famous.

And Katie . . . well, I already explained why it can't be her. But in case my boss thinks I reached this conclusion because of hormones, I had her story checked too, and she totally doesn't fit the profile. First off, Katie is all woman, and most hackers are not. Second, she has a well-documented family history through her aristocratic English father and an Indian maharaja grandfather on her mother's side. Your average hacker-for-hire millionaire is only rich because hacking made him that way, not because he was born into it like Katie. Plus, I believe her when she says she chose Carlisle to improve her chances of acceptance at the local university's optical physics program—aka laser science—the best in the country.

That leaves two other students on my list: one male, one female. I got so sidetracked by Katie for a while there, my intel on them is sketchy at best. All I know about the girl is that her family has been in the mining business for generations. What I know about the dude is that I *cannot* stand him and hope like hell he's the one.

I'm looking over some notes I've made—indecipherable, of course—when I go to adjust my glasses and find them gone. In my defense, when you have perfect vision, it's easy not to notice you're missing your fake glasses for three and a half periods.

Oh, that's right. I took them off to clean right about the time the fire alarm went off. I remember leaving them on the desk before we all filed out, but now that I think about it, they weren't there when we returned. I was so focused on Katie's disappearing act, I hadn't noticed they were gone. Who the hell would take my glasses? Whoever it was will discover there's zero prescription in them, just as Bunker suspected. Maybe he grabbed them for me. Or . . . could that be the reason Katie went missing? Did she notice I wasn't wearing them and went back for them?

Nah, that's crazy. One—she'd have to care that much about me. Two—I'd have to believe I was something special to think she'd run back into a potentially burning building just so I'd be able to see. Not that you could blame me for thinking I'm all that, considering how these girls are scoping me right now. As long as Bunker isn't around, I'll admit I have always had a strong game with the girls. All that gym time required of my CIA training hasn't hurt it either, but damn, these girls are jockin' me. Is this what they feel like *all* the time? Because it's making me a little uncomfortable.

And apparently my glasses really are a powerful cover. I wasn't wearing them in the photo that girl tweeted, either, and a few hundred girls thought I looked good enough to retweet. I wish Bunk was here so I could tell him Clark Kent knew what he was doing, but I need to eighty-six the suspect-hunting, and retrieve the backup pair from my locker.

The theory about Katie having them is a bust. I pass her table as I leave the cafeteria, but she doesn't even look up from her copy of *Pride and Prejudice.* You'd think a British girl would have already read it, but maybe I'm just stereotyping. Anyway, Katie might be the only girl in the place who isn't staring me down right now.

"Uh, excuse me, Pee-tah."

Or maybe I spoke too soon.

"Katie, I didn't even see you there."

Smooth. I'm sure she bought that one. You'd have to be blindfolded or have your head covered with a dark burlap sack to miss Katie Carmichael. I've had both of those things happen at the same time, and even under those conditions I'd probably still notice her. Yes, she's that gorgeous.

"Are you enjoying your fifteen minutes?" she asks.

"Um, what?" Also smooth.

She smiles as though we're sharing an inside joke, but I don't have a clue, and apparently she isn't going to let me in on it.

"I have something for you," she says, reaching into her bag.

Wow. She really *did* go back for my glasses. "I was wondering where they were. That was really cool of you to risk—"

"Your half of the bill," she says, handing me a piece of paper. "If you recall, we agreed to split the costs of homecoming. I'd buy the tickets and dinner and you'd pay me back. It's been two weeks and I thought perhaps you'd forgotten."

Her tone indicates she thought no such thing. Her tone indicates she thinks I'm not only a loser who'd dump her the day before homecoming, but that I'd actually stick her with the tab for it. And she's right, except I didn't intentionally scam on the bill. In my obsession with finding the hacker, and oh yeah, trying to get over *her,* I just spaced it.

"Oh, snap, I really did forget. I swear. Here, let me just give you the full amount."

"I don't need the full amount," she says, crushing my grand gesture. "I went to the dance and had a very nice evening. My date turned out to be as adept on the dance floor as he is in the engineering lab," she adds, crushing my heart.

There's pretty much nothing left to say after that, so I take the rejected half of my money and walk away, certain I can feel the death rays her eyes must be shooting into my back. But when I turn around to get one last look at her, Katie is engrossed in her book, as though I'd never been there.

CHAPTER 5

Once I leave the cafeteria in search of my spare pair of glasses, I hear a whistling sound coming from the short hall leading to the main front entrance. Since Carlisle Academy won some big award for energy efficiency, there should be no drafts anywhere in the building. It must be coming from an open door.

Pretty much only visitors use this door, so it's no big deal that it's been recently opened. But the hydraulic door closer should have fastened shut when the last person went out. And if it was ajar for more than thirty seconds, an alarm should have gone off. Carlisle takes this stuff more seriously than airport TSA during an orange-level terrorist threat, so something isn't right. Someone must have tinkered with it.

I find a small piece of paper at the bottom of the door, folded a couple of times to make it thick enough to keep the door from closing, but making the fact that it isn't closed almost imperceptible. When I unfold the paper, I see it's a bit thicker, more like the weight of a postcard; matte white on one side, shiny red on the other, and embossed with a white abstract design that seems vaguely familiar. I backtrack to the main office around the corner to get more information.

The second thing I did upon my arrival at Carlisle was to befriend the office staff. Dodson might think she runs the show, but it's her assistant that makes her look so good, and the assistant's assistant who keeps the whole thing running. I stay on his good side with items from what I call my asset acquisitions cache, or bribe box. Things like a Cuban cigar my "mother," a diplomatic attaché, brought back from the inaugural diplomatic trip after the US embargo was lifted. Or just last week, I gave him a pair of Denver Broncos tickets—just about the hardest NFL seats to get outside of Green Bay or Washington, DC—when my "father" suddenly couldn't use them.

My official CIA dossier indicates I have no mother and father, that they are both deceased, which is the truth. They went to Kenya for their tenth wedding anniversary and died during a big storm when their van tried to cross a washed-out road. My parents left for the airport one day, and that was the last time I ever saw them. At first I imagined they were still out there somewhere, and I made up stories of why they couldn't get back to me. It made it easier to deal.

But then I grew up. Now my parents are like my assets, and the stories I make up about them help me do my job. I won't lie—it sucks to have no family. Actually, it hurts like hell. But having no one in the world who gives a damn about me makes for a perfect CIA operative. It's probably the reason Rogers pulled me out of the foster system—

that and my hacking skills—and made me her first Early Bird operative. If I'm ever caught, the bad guys will have no one to use as leverage against me.

Getting fired permanently would suck because the agency is the closest thing I've had to a family since I lost my real one.

When I get to the office, I find only one person behind the bulletproof window. Carlisle is a few miles outside the nearest town, yet administration treats security as though the campus is in the middle of the toughest big-city neighborhood. Some might call it overkill. I call it smart planning. There are no metal detectors at the entrance, like there were at all of my old schools—can't make exclusive Carlisle feel like it's a dangerous place to be—but everything else about the security is top-notch.

Well, maybe not right at this moment, because Dodson's assistant's assistant has his back to the closed guest window, engaged in what must be a pretty serious phone call from the look of his body language. His stance is like a soldier's at ease: feet shoulder-width apart, his free hand resting on the small of his back, palm facing me, except when he briefly holds it on top of his head. I'm guessing he hasn't been watching the hallway, the window, or the monitor for the security camera trained on the front door. When I push the service buzzer, he turns, startled, and quickly ends his phone call.

"What's up, Jonesy?" I ask when he unlocks the window and slides it open. "Broncos handle their business yesterday or what?"

"You missed a good one, brother," he says, his tone

giving away nothing about the conversation I'd just interrupted. "I damn near went broke on stadium beer, but that's what I get for celebrating a little too hard. Tell your dad how much I appreciate those tickets. I took mine and made him the happiest man in Denver."

Maybe it's because I was just thinking about my orphan status, but Jonesy's game report makes me both bummed and happy at the same time. I lost my parents nearly half my lifetime ago. Too many memories of my dad have already faded, but I'm glad I gave Jonesy a chance to make some memories with his.

"What can I do you for?"

"I have chemistry next and just realized I've lost my lab notebook. I know I'm not supposed to get supplies from the office, but—"

"Not a problem, my man," Jonesy says, getting up and heading for the supply closet in back. In the minute he's gone, I'm able to sneak a look at the visitor sign-in screen.

Hmm. Not good.

I put the sign-in tablet back where I found it just as Jonesy returns with the notebook and an industrial-sized bottle of Tylenol, explaining, "For my pounding headache. A little too much game-day celebration last night."

"I know you only stock these notebooks for teachers. I can pay you for it," I say, handing him a five-dollar bill, but for the second time in the past ten minutes, my money is rejected.

"Don't worry about it. Just don't tell anyone or I'll have fifty kids up in here asking for stuff. And watch it with the *Jonesy*. Only my friends call me that, and the Carlisle

Official Handbook says you can't be my friend. I'm still in my new-hire probationary period; gotta keep up appearances, Mr. Smith."

"Right, Mr. Jones."

I thank him for the notebook just as the bell rings. I head for my locker, thinking about what I saw in the visitor's log. Or what I didn't see. I don't like the fact that we've had no visitors since fifth period—some doctor to meet with his kid's teacher—and yet the door has been propped open for nearly an hour. It was probably a student who went out front to sneak a contraband smoke break, but why didn't the alarm go off after thirty seconds? The folded paper kept the door from latching closed, but maybe not open enough to trigger the alarm. And about that paper— I have this nagging feeling that I've seen the design before. Not sure why the image should make me feel uneasy, but it does. It's probably the hacker in me—I can't stand an unsolved puzzle.

After I fight with my always-stuck locker door and grab my backup glasses from the shelf, I see Bunker passing by and nod at him. Katie also goes by but I do nothing, mostly because she hasn't even looked in my direction. She knows exactly where my locker is, so she has to be working hard not to notice me. Again, not that I blame her.

Then, I see the scary blond freshman coming down the hall and there's no question whether she notices me. She slows her pace as she nears my locker. If she comes over, I'm going out of nerd-boy character long enough to tell her I'm not interested and to back the hell off. In fact, I'll tell her exactly what I think about her whole Twitter game. But she continues past me, calling out, "Hey there, prettyboy," as she lowers her eyeglasses a little, winking at me over them. "Your picture in the student directory didn't do you justice, so I did."

Wait—aren't those *my* glasses?

I'm about to chase her down when Mr. Velasquez, my chem teacher, ushers me into his classroom, saying, "Don't want to be late, do we, Mr. Smith?" forcing me to deal with my number-one fan later.

When I walk into the room, I see Carlisle's resident douche—and my fifth possible suspect—at the lab table in back of the class. I always sit in the last row, and I always sit at that table.

"Excuse me, but would you mind going to your own table now?" I ask him as pleasantly as possible. "Class is about to start."

"As a matter of fact, I do mind. Think I'll sit here today."

Being able to seriously jack up a dude doesn't quite go with the nerdy persona I've created, but if anyone ever makes me go out of character in the name of a justified ass-kicking, it will be Duke Duncan. Nice gets you nowhere with this guy.

"Outta my seat," I tell him, hoping a stern voice will be enough.

Duncan looks incredulous, as though I've asked him to do something impossible, like be a decent human being. "Make me."

Oh, don't tempt me. But I make like Gandhi and try the peaceful approach. "Will this do it?" I hand him the bill Jonesy just refused.

"That'll do just fine," he says, grabbing the fiver. Finally, someone who doesn't turn down my money, even mad-rich Duncan. "But I would have done it for free. Watching your expression when you see this would have been payment enough, considering your hate of any and all social interaction."

Duncan's a douche in English Lit and German, too, where I'm also his favorite target despite my efforts to avoid him. He's right about me keeping a low profile, but in his case, my aversion is to him specifically.

"See what?" I ask, not able to help myself.

Duncan gets out of my seat as he hands me his phone, where I see the same photo Bunker showed me this morning.

"Yeah, I already know about that," I say, handing it back to him.

"No, take a closer look," Duncan instructs. "Scroll down some."

I do, and see that the photo is now tagged #Prettyboy. I scroll down some more and see a bunch of comments like:

Oooh, he really is a #Prettyboy. Grabby hands!
Yum, #Prettyboy. Want.
Does anyone have #Prettyboy's number?
Forget his number. I need #Prettyboy's address.

But wait, there's more. There are now 5,083 retweets. How is that even possible since first period? I scroll up the page, terrified to look but knowing I have to. And yes, it gets worse. Much worse.

"Now *that's* the look I would have given up your seat

for, no charge," Duncan says, grabbing his phone before I can drop it as I nearly go into shock. Maybe I should have reported this to Rogers after all. Maybe now it's time to panic.

#Prettyboy is trending in Denver.

CHAPTER 6

No matter how trivial his boss thinks the mission, or how exclusive the boarding school he's enrolled in, or how bucolic the campus, having his cover blown is the absolute worst thing that can happen to a covert operative.

The only thing keeping me from a complete and total meltdown right now is the fact that the hacker doesn't know who I am, what I look like, or that I'm at Carlisle. I'm hoping whoever he works for doesn't either, and that if they do, they're too busy selling weapons to terrorists or laundering cyber-stolen money through the Cayman Islands to check their Twitter timelines, even if *I* can't stop checking the rapidly rising number of #Prettyboy tweets.

Unless the hacker really *is* Duncan, and he's known all along who I am, and he got that girl to take the photo and he's behind my picture going viral so quickly and . . . Okay, time to slow my roll. None of that makes sense. Even if Duncan *is* the hacker, he obviously knows who I am, and doesn't need to out me or start a Twitter campaign to reveal my identity to his employers. I'm just getting way paranoid, even for a spy.

Still, I need to get rid of that photo ASAP. I won't be

able to do that while sitting in a chem lab for the next fifty minutes, pretending I care about the properties of matter while each retweet further compromises my search, not to mention my safety. I decide to skip out before the second bell rings and head for the door, but Mr. Velasquez closes off my escape route.

"Going somewhere, Mr. Smith?"

"No, sir," I say, slipping my phone into my pocket. Don't need to give him a reason to take it from me. I'll need it during class to clandestinely hack Twitter and take down Blondie's tweet and the thousands of retweets it has generated. It won't fix the problem, but it'll buy me time while I come up with a better solution. That's one of many reasons I prefer a back-row seat. Stealth operations.

But Mr. Velasquez has other plans.

"Good, because you won't want to miss the spectacular treat I have in store today, and you're going to be my assistant since you're already up here."

"Um, but Mr. Velasquez, I really need—"

"—to find out what you get when you combine red phosphorus, sulfur, and potassium chlorate? Unless you already know the answer, Mr. Smith, you'll remain right here with me."

"You get fire, sir. Those are the three main elements that make up the head on a matchstick," I say, before heading to my lab table.

"Not so fast, Mr. Smith."

"But I knew the answer. You said—"

"I didn't think you actually would, but it's clear I've chosen the right person to help me demonstrate today's experiment. But first, erase that whiteboard for me while

I explain the hypothesis and experiment to your not-as-chemically-gifted classmates."

While Velasquez drones on about physical versus chemical properties, I realize why the abstract design on that piece of paper is so familiar. Erasing the board, I quickly take the paper from my pocket and sniff. Sulfur. It's the cover from a matchbook, the kind you rarely find outside restaurants and hotels, and hardly even there anymore, at least not in this country. But in parts of Europe where smoking is still like a religion, matchbooks are everywhere. Now I remember where I've seen that design. Even though it went by me at ninety kilometers per hour, I'm pretty sure it was the logo of a hotel I passed on my ride from the airport through Kiev.

Ukraine.

One of the first things you learn in spy school: there are no coincidences.

The realization that someone from *that* operation might be inside Carlisle just about knocks me on my ass. I drop the eraser and brace myself against Velasquez's lab table as a sudden wave of dizziness and nausea hits me.

"Mr. Smith, you don't look so great. Are you well?"

"I . . . think . . . so."

"If you're to be my assistant, you need to *know* so. I can't have you blowing up my sixth period," Velasquez says, getting a couple of laughs from the class, along with a *Yeah, don't ruin that Prettyboy face* from some girl. I can't tell which one because right now, I can barely talk.

"I'm fine, sir," I lie, hoping this will play out the way I expect.

Velasquez looks skeptical, but hands me a slip of paper. "Fetch these items from the supply room."

Just what I hoped he would say. I've bought myself a couple of minutes to do something I should have done an hour ago.

I check the classroom on the other side of the supply room, which is really more like a big closet, and find it empty. That's right; Ms. Flagler was supposed to take both her biology classes on a field trip to the museum today. Perfect. I won't be interrupted by someone sent to fetch supplies for a bio experiment.

I never linked the hacker to Marchuk until now, because we were able to shut down his operation despite my screwup. And with his former boss in a shallow grave somewhere, I just figured the hacker had moved on to the next illegal arms supplier with a job opening. But it's possible the hacker is still tied to someone in the Marchuk operation. How else does a hotel matchbook get halfway around the world from Ukraine to Colorado? There is a single Ukrainian student on campus, but she cleared my suspect list because she's a junior in her third year at Carlisle. We're in the same English Lit class.

As I close the adjacent supply-room door behind me, I tell myself she's behind the propped-open door, but still I begin placing the phone call that has become a whole lot more important than just reporting how I'm all over the internet. Like I said, the matchbook can't be a coincidence. My intel says neither the girl nor her family have returned to Ukraine since they arrived here three years ago. And I know from cyberstalking him that the hacker left Ukraine the same day I did. So who carries a hotel matchbook around in his pocket for seven months? No one.

Who *would* have a matchbook from that hotel? Some- one who only recently arrived from Ukraine, that's who.

Weird. My phone is showing zero bars, even though there's a cell tower an eighth of a mile up the road. Luck- ily, there's a landline hanging on the wall of the supply room. I punch in Rogers's number, but just as my call be- gins to ring, the line goes dead. Pressing the receiver but- ton a couple of times doesn't make it come back to life.

I check my phone again. Still no bars. All the metal storage cabinets could be blocking electromagnetic ra- dio waves from the cell tower, like when you can't make a call from an elevator. Since Carlisle went all out on their security, maybe that includes securing a supply room full of combustible chemicals. Maybe the room is one big safety cabinet and the walls are lined with eighteen- gauge steel. It's a stretch, but I'd rather that be the case than the other theory I'm trying not to come up with, which has to do with the hacker's specialty—communications. He's a modern-day phreak—a genius at all things tele- phony.

I try Ms. Flagler's room. No cell reception in here, either. Okay, this ain't good. And soon, Mr. Velasquez is going to send someone to see what's taking me so long. It's a won- der he hasn't done it already. But he's going to have to wait a bit longer.

I head for the hallway in search of a working phone, and just as I turn the doorknob, I hear what sounds like a scream—piercing at first, then muffled—come from my chem class.

The screamer was quieted quickly, but I heard enough to know someone in my class is terrified. It stops me in my tracks. Do I head for the hall and a phone, or go back to chem and help? Before I can really think through my decision, I'm walking quickly through the bio lab and back into the supply room. I open the door just a crack. What I see makes my blood run cold.

There are two masked men in front of the classroom, both wearing the uniform of black-ops soldiers everywhere: cargo pants, t-shirt, boots, tactical belt. The first bad guy has one hand covering the mouth of the girl who must have screamed, and I'm guessing the heavy-looking bag in his other hand isn't holding a picnic lunch.

"Look, I don't want any more of that screaming nonsense because there's no reason for it," the other bad guy explains in a thick New York accent. He obviously doesn't understand how two guys dropping through the ceiling might worry most people. "I can promise no one will get hurt if you only cooperate. We're thieves, not killers."

My classmates are probably hoping that story is true, but I'm not buying it.

Mr. Velasquez isn't convinced, either. As Bad Guy #2 reaches into the back of his waistband, probably for a weapon, my teacher tries to tackle him. Heroic, but a very bad move. These thieves are probably professionals to have gotten this far past Carlisle's security measures. And Velasquez is a chem teacher.

Oh no. Now he's a chem teacher in an expertly applied choke hold. Before I can even process what's happening, the bad guy is already done with Mr. Velasquez, who he lets slump to the floor, unconscious. Or worse.

I try not to completely lose my lunch as I move through the biology classroom and head for the nearest exit.

CHAPTER 7

Out in the hallway, everything is quiet, as though there aren't two very scary men in sixth-period chemistry holding seventeen people hostage. But you learn in the spy trade to assume nothing is as it seems, so I move quietly toward the main door. If this is happening anywhere else in the building, and all the phone lines are down, our only chance is for me to get out and find help. I stay close to the wall of lockers in case I need to suddenly take cover by running into the restroom, a janitor's supply closet, or worst case, one of the classrooms.

Truth? I'm tempted to duck into one of those places and hide out until these people get what they want and leave. Right now I'd much rather be just a kid who is having the worst day of his senior year than a highly trained CIA operative—with a potentially blown cover, thanks to that stupid photo—who has a duty to *do* something.

I know what they said about being thieves, but a guy who can take high-school kids as hostages—and take out a teacher who was only trying to protect them—cannot be trusted to tell the truth. And like I said, that Ukrainian matchbook can't be random. It's safer to work from multiple assumptions. Considering their obvious infiltration skills and the weight and size of that tactical gear bag they were carrying, this is what I'm thinking so far:

1. They're truly thieves and have come to steal something really valuable.
2. They're lost thieves and have somehow mistaken Carlisle for the Denver Mint.
3. They're hostiles here to kill me.

Yeah, putting it all in a mental list like that makes me feel sooo much better. If I get out of this alive, I'll be sure to tell my Threat Assessment 101 instructor at Langley how great that worked to help me stay focused and in control.

As I move down the hall, I peek through the small glass window on the doors of the two nearest classrooms and find that everything is normal: the teachers are in command of the rooms, and the only thing students are fighting off is post-lunch sleepiness. That means no one else heard the scream. It might also mean the men really *are* thieves—possibly combat-armed thieves—but nothing more. No other classrooms are being taken over by force.

I hold on to that idea as I make my way to the main entrance. I consider going to the office, but what good would that do? The thieves—or more likely the hacker who must be working with them—have already cut the landlines and blocked our cell phone signals, which means I need to get out of the building. No one in the office can help us now.

Then I remember the undercover security guards who

pretend to be part of the maintenance and grounds crew. They're probably outside somewhere, clueless to the breach. We need the police, but until I can somehow get word to them, those guards can be a first line of defense. Despite their best efforts to look like the kind of employees no one notices, I'm certain the school hired both men because they're ex-military. They are recent additions to the security system that is so appealing to the type of parents who send their kids to Carlisle. I need to find those guys.

As I reach Corridor A, my heart rate begins to slow to a pace that might not kill me. I'm in the homestretch. My way out is in view, and just beyond the main entrance is the school office. I'm glad to see there are no teachers or students freaking out at Jonesy's window. I quickly cover the fifteen yards between me and the entrance, but as soon as I turn down the short corridor leading to the front door, the same one that had been propped open by the matchbook cover, I see that I'm too late.

The bulletproof, double-thick windows are already obscured. Instead of sunshine, blue sky, and the Boulder foothills, I only see cold, gray metal.

The gunmen must have hacked the security system and lowered the steel shutters over the front doors. Probably over the rear and side entrances, too. And except for the people in my chem class, no one even knows they're in trouble yet.

I stand there a second, still trying to hold on to the idea that these guys really are thieves. And it isn't just wishful thinking. Most everyone at Carlisle comes from families who are rich, powerful, connected, or all of the above. It's possible these guys *are* here to steal—not some*thing,* but some*one*. This might be a kidnapping. They might be here for Joel Easter, ransoming him for the encryption technology his father is working on at NIST. Or they've come for the fourth new student, that girl whose mother literally owns a gold mine in the foothills outside of town.

But that's only a guess. Since I'm not sure what their true goal is, I need to assume it's bad. And now that I'm trapped inside with everyone else, I need to be as prepared as possible to fight them. First stop is my locker for a few emergency supplies. Only problem? It's back in Corridor B, just outside my chem class. I retrace my steps, moving more quickly than before, since this time I may not get as lucky going undetected. At some point, if the men really are thieves, they'll have to leave my chemistry class to steal whatever it is they're here for—unless there are more than two of them.

That thought nearly stops me in my tracks. I have to push myself to keep moving.

As I turn the tumbler to the last number on my combination lock, I seriously regret not oiling my locker, because of course it jams up on me. No choice, I need those supplies. I bang my fist against the locker door, grab the pack the second it pops open, shut the door, and run like hell twenty feet to the alcove leading to the boys' bathroom.

I take a look around the corner and see it—my locker door didn't shut completely. It's only open a hair, imperceptible unless you're looking for it. But people skilled in stealth infiltration will look for it. Can't go back now, can't leave the alcove, so I stand there, waiting for what I know is coming.

And there it is. The sound of a doorknob turning, then

my chemistry classroom's door opening. I don't hear any footsteps, probably because the thief is wearing rubber-soled shoes. But I know he's coming. There's a collapsible baton in my bag, at the very bottom, hidden beneath a bunch of harmless-looking stuff in case of a surprise locker check. But it's the only weapon I have that might stop this guy. And he's close, even though I still can't hear him. The second I shove my hand into my backpack to feel around for the baton, my hand rattles one of my makeshift, locker-safe weapons—a sock full of ball bearings.

Oh no. Did he hear that? Now I don't even have the element of surprise. Okay. I can either run, fight, or . . . hope he doesn't know who I am. If he really is here for me, I'm screwed. But if he's a thief, as far as this guy knows, I'm just a kid in a hallway. That's a normal thing in a high school, right? I'm just Peter Smith. I'll just act like—

That's when my near panic attack is interrupted by a buzzing over the PA system.

It's Headmistress Dodson.

"Students, faculty, and staff—I am calling an unscheduled assembly. Please report to the auditorium, in ABC formation, beginning at one o'clock."

Her message is brief, but long enough for me to know the assembly is not the kind we've rehearsed along with fire drills. Dodson is trying to hold it together, and probably no one else detected it but me, but her Voice-of-God tone was gone. It had crept just a step higher. Dodson is terrified.

CHAPTER 8

I hold my breath and peek around the corner again. No one there. Guess the announcement sent him back into the room. I make a dash for the office again. Dodson obviously knows what's going on, but if she's afraid, there must be hostiles in the office, too. I have to figure out a way to find out what she knows without getting either of us killed.

Back in Corridor A, there's no activity in the hall, but the service window is still open and I can hear murmurs of conversation. I drop to the floor and crawl until I'm just beneath the window, where I hear an unfamiliar female voice.

"Is this all of your office staff? Is everyone accounted for?"

"Yes, we're all here," Dodson says. "It's just the four of us."

I run through the list of office staff. There are usually five: Dodson, her assistant, the registrar, the financial officer, and Jonesy. Since Dodson doesn't explain, I'm guessing someone called in sick or took a vacation day. But I'm hoping all five were here at some point, someone got away, and Dodson is smart enough not to mention that fifth employee.

"What was that about the ABC formation?" the woman asks in a Southern accent, maybe Mississippi or Louisiana, but only a hint. She hasn't lived there for a long time.

"It's a staggered movement plan, so we don't have the whole school moving to one location at once," Dodson explains, sounding calmer than she did just a minute ago on the PA system. "Students and staff move according to the corridor they're currently in and where we've directed them to go. The auditorium is on Corridor B, so those students on all three floors will head out first. Corridor A will begin moving two minutes later. C is last. All of our clocks are digital and centralized. Everyone should be in the auditorium within six minutes."

"You run a tight ship," the woman says, and I can imagine Dodson smiling at the compliment if she wasn't being held against her will. "Knowing two of us are on the inside should help ease the panic."

Um, what?

"Yes, I agree, though I don't expect there will be much of that," Dodson says. "Given our student body—who their parents are—we drill them on this procedure every semester. Just this morning, we had a false alarm—but we take all possible threats very seriously until they are refuted or eliminated—and our students handled it perfectly. They may even think this assembly is related to that."

I still don't know what they're talking about, but it's clear Dodson is not afraid of whoever's in the office. In fact, she seems almost hospitable, by Dodson standards.

"Very smart, ma'am. At this point, we believe there are two suspects currently on the campus, though we've not yet ascertained their location. We have units outside along the perimeter, and I'm sure these people know that. In case the suspects are already in the building, we don't want to alarm them into doing something stupid by bringing heavy forces inside."

I don't need to see the woman to know who she is. That was total cop speak. My relief is almost overwhelming. I'm about to reveal myself, but Dodson asks a few good questions that make me hesitate.

"But why come here? Why not keep taking the road out of town, or up into the mountains? Or take the highway into Denver, where they could get lost in the crowd? You don't think they're here for one of our students, do you?"

"As far as we know, they aren't after anyone here. They're just looking for somewhere to lie low. We pursued them from that bank at the edge of town, the one just before Broadway turns into Highway Thirty-Six," the officer says. "There isn't much between there and here. Carlisle had the bad luck of being the place they decided to take cover in once they knew we were in pursuit."

That explains why Dodson sounded so scared during the announcement—she must have just learned bank robbers were hiding out here. Or at least people who she believes are bank robbers.

I'm still holding out hope that's who they really are. It's a better scenario than what my gut is telling me.

"But they passed several homes on big sprawling acreages, even a few ranches, before Carlisle," Dodson says, sounding tired, as though she realized the minute she said it that it didn't really matter at this point.

"It's the middle of the day, those homes are probably empty. And the ranches . . . Well, those places don't offer what your school does."

"What's that?"

I know the answer before it's spoken. It explains why the gunmen are holding my classmates in place.

"Hostages, and plenty of them."

There is a collective gasp from Dodson and the staff, who have been silent until now. Dang. The officer could have lied a little, maybe said she didn't know why they chose Carlisle, even if Dodson and the others no doubt expected that would be the reason. This situation calls for a softer touch. I sure hope this cop isn't also the hostage negotiator.

"The students and staff may wonder about the change in protocol, since our normal procedure is to hold in place until the building is cleared by your people."

"Yes, that is S.O.P.—uh, standard operating procedure, ma'am—but this case is a little different since there is the possibility that the suspects are inside the building," the officer explains. "It would be safer to have the students in one place until we can find these men."

"But there are only two of you, Detective Andrews," Dodson says. "That could take a while."

Good point, Dodson. If the police have tracked bank robbers to the school, and know they're here, where's the cavalry? Standard operating procedure is to move in immediately if a school is being threatened. The halls should be crawling with cops. Letting five hundred people move through a building hijacked by bank robbers without heavy police escort doesn't seem right. The classroom doors are made of steel, and contain bulletproof windows, which Dodson has no doubt explained. She's right. Everyone would be safer staying where they are until the building is cleared.

And about these guys being bank robbers. That might explain the gunmen's infiltration skills and tactical gear— in the Hollywood version of a bank heist. In *real* life, the average bank robber does so on impulse and out of desperation, usually some loser meth-head needing a hit. He won't wear a ski mask or even a ball cap pulled low over his eyes because he probably didn't plan to rob a bank that day—the opportunity just presents itself and he takes it. He hits a bank where he can do just as Dodson suggested: get on the nearest highway and blend into the crowd long before the police arrive.

"My partner and I will accompany you and your staff to the auditorium and hopefully provide a calming presence as you explain that the school is under lockdown," the officer says without really addressing Dodson's concerns. "It would be best if we get there before they start moving. We want this assembly to seem as normal as possible."

I hear movement in the office, and then Andrews says, "Oh, it's best you leave everything here. I know you want to contact your loved ones, but we don't want the suspects to intercept any phone calls which might give them information about our presence here. The faster we can resolve this, the faster we can all get out of here and home to our families."

I know I'm only a year out of training, but this sounds

like a pretty crap plan to me. I'm about to stand up and tell them so, when Andrews's partner speaks.

"I recently lost someone dear to me in similar circumstance, Ms. Dodson. It weighs heavily on me today, so trust that I will not fail. Detective Andrews and I have situation under control."

It isn't what he says that keeps me crouched below the window. It's *how* he says it. He's trying to suppress it, but I detect an accent that explains why he didn't say "*a* similar circumstance" or "*the* situation."

It may be Russian, but my money's on Ukrainian.

CHAPTER 9

Now it makes sense why that first cop, the one calling herself Detective Andrews, didn't try to soften the hard news—because she isn't really a cop. She's a terrorist or black-market arms dealer, probably both, considering who her partner is.

It isn't just the guy's accent that seals it for me. It's what he said about losing someone "in similar circumstance." Marchuk Sr. was a traitor to his country and a longtime regular on Interpol's most wanted list, so not a lot of people miss him. The only one who does is supposed to be dead.

It wasn't a fluke that those hostiles chose my classroom to make their incursion. It's not a coincidence the hacker is helping them.

That girl took my picture fifteen hours ago, probably posted it straight after. It went viral between first and sixth period. Only two hundred people had seen it before first bell. Marchuk must have been one of them, which means the whole time we assumed he was dead, he has been watching, probably from somewhere close, Canada or Mexico maybe. Hell, he may have been stateside the whole time. It's a great place to hide from assassins who are even more afraid than he is to be caught on our turf. Playing dead and just waiting to pick off any member of our Ukraine team that he could identify. I must be the first.

Lucky me.

Surely the CIA had some intelligence on his resurfacing. Doesn't matter that I'm basically a burned spy, a heads-up from Rogers on *that* little development would have been nice.

I hear the shuffling of feet inside the office. They must be leaving for the auditorium, which means I don't have a lot of time to put together a plan. I crouch low and move as quickly as I can away from the office and into the closest alcove, out of sight but still with an eye on them thanks to the periscope from my supply stash. From around the corner, I see the two hostiles are dressed in street clothes, like detectives, I suppose. I'm able to count four members of the office staff, including Dodson. All women. Jonesy's headache must have sent him home. He must have gotten out just before the hostiles arrived. I'm glad someone did.

As soon as they're out of sight, I run back around the corner, into the office, and begin checking every drawer, every purse hanging on the back of a chair, hoping to find a working cell phone. It must be the hacker who cut the landlines, but I'm hoping it was only my cell phone they blocked. They wouldn't risk anyone in the building using their cells to call the police, but at this point, I'm guessing the only people who know there are bad guys in the building are in my chem class.

No luck. None of the office staff's cell phones work either. The hostiles have somehow blocked the nearest cell-tower signal. I shove one of the phones into my pocket just in case the signal blocker is close, and the phone might work in another part of the building. Next, I start checking every computer in the office for network connectivity. I know it's probably useless, but it gives me something to do while I think through the facts I know so far.

My chem lab must be the only individual class they took over. They're probably still in there now. In order for the hostiles to take over each class in the same manner, they would have had to assign at least one agent to thirty classrooms, so that each breach happened simultaneously. They'd need another platoon of agents. While I was in Ukraine, I'd only counted a team of nine, and after the raid-gone-bad, our side left theirs nine men short. Or so we thought. Obviously Marchuk got away. He must have taken on some new team members.

I'm hoping there are only the four of them—two in chemistry, Andrews, and the grieving son.

Four operatives would probably be overkill if their original plan had worked: infiltrate Mr. Velasquez's room, extract me, and get out. My good luck of being in the supply room meant everyone else's bad luck. Now they're going to use all those hostages Andrews spoke of to draw me out. Just thinking about it makes me want to puke. But I got work to do.

Not a single one of these office computers is online. I have to get help some other way. If I'm right and there are only four of them, this may be my only chance to move freely through the school. It's a long shot, but maybe they haven't put the security doors down on the rear exits. Since

I'm closest to Corridor C and it's the farthest point from the auditorium, I make my way to that exit first.

Like the side and back exits of a movie theater, the rear doors at Carlisle can't be opened from the outside during the day. They can only be used to exit the building, and only in an emergency. If they're opened, an alarm will go off and the hostiles will know someone has made their escape. They'll likely assume that that someone is me, but it's a risk I'll have to take. I just hope the alarm won't set them off and make them do something stupid to one of the kids in chem or one of the office staff in the auditorium. I couldn't take it if they hurt someone else just because they're after me.

I'm feeling hopeful when, from the end of the hall, I can see blue sky through the window of the south door. I run hard toward the light.

All that risk assessment I just did turns out to be useless. There is no alarm because the door doesn't open, no matter how many times I throw myself against it. Hoping the signal is better here, I check the bars on my phone.

Nothing.

I'm getting jittery; the panic starting to set in. I'm feeling a lot like every time I met yet another foster family for the first time, wondering if they'd be decent people, or if I'd be better off back on the street, already planning my escape before the social worker drove away.

To push it down, I make my way back around to the other arm of the U, taking the stairwell to the second floor, running through all three corridors and back downstairs again, checking both phones all along the way. Once I get around to the other rear exit, I find this door is locked too, and the signal is blocked on both phones here as well.

Then I remember the window-breaker in my backpack. It's a little orange hammer with a pointy metal end and a blade like a box cutter in its neck, designed to break water-jammed windows and cut stuck seat belts to escape a sinking car. You can buy them anywhere, but they make a perfect spy tool. I can feel the jitters beginning to subside as I pull off my blazer and use it to shield my eyes from shattering glass.

That precaution proves just as useless as my earlier risk assessment. The glass doesn't shatter. All my hammer does is leave an impression, something like a bullet would leave in bulletproof glass. It would take a sledgehammer to break this window. I peer through the glass, hoping there's someone out there—maybe one of the soldiers-turned-school-employees—anyone, really, who might notice me and understand my plea for help. But the only thing I see out there is the student parking lot and cottonwood trees just beginning to yellow.

I slide down the door into a sitting position, feeling déjà vu. Yes, I've been here before, in this exact moment, except it was in Ukraine, just before I passed out. I want to give up, curl myself into a ball and hope that somehow help will come soon, like it did then. All that training they gave me at Langley doesn't make me feel like anything other than what I am—a scared kid who wishes he'd never said yes to the Company's offer.

If I'd said no, I'd probably be in jail right now serving a sentence for hacking the National Security Agency, and not a juvie sentence, either. I would be doing some real time. But at least there'd be no chance of having blood on my hands. Or maybe I'd have found a way to hack myself out of it—destroyed all the FBI's evidence before my trial. If I'd said no, maybe I wouldn't blame my latest foster parents for not being my real parents. I wouldn't be such an ass about it. I'd be grateful they said yes to me. I'd only be worried about grades and making varsity track. Maybe I'd be going out with a really dope girl.

But I didn't say no.

And in ninety seconds, all of Carlisle is about to be rounded up in one place, making it easier for Marchuk and his team to control them.

I said yes, so now it's my job to stop the bad guys. I'm not sure how I'm going to do that by myself with what's in my backpack, but one thing I can do right now is keep everyone from reaching the auditorium. Even if I don't know how to beat the hostiles, I can at least make it hard for them.

I run like hell for the office and arrive forty-five seconds later, nearly out of breath.

When I switch on the PA system, I'm so relieved to find it's still working. Hopefully, people won't think I'm some panting, raving lunatic, if they even know who I am at all. About ten people in all of Carlisle have a clue who Peter Smith is, thanks to my skills at flying under the radar. No, I need to assume another persona if I want people to hear me.

"Listen up, Carlisle. This is Prettyboy. Abort the assembly. Repeat: Abort the assembly. Follow Red-Level procedures—now! Dodson, those two people with you are not real cops.

There are no bank robbers on the loose, just the two hit men with you and two others holding sixth-period chem hostage. They're here to kill me. Don't believe anything they—"

The audio suddenly cuts out. I'm only talking to myself.

CHAPTER 10

About ten seconds after the PA system dies, I receive confirmation that my plan worked. I guess it took that long for people to grasp what I said or wonder whether I was crazy, but they must have decided to believe the shit has hit the fan, because suddenly I hear screaming and shouting coming in muffled waves through the corridor, which remains empty. I hope that's because the teachers are following my direction and have gone to Red-Level protocol, locking down their classrooms so they can only be opened from the inside. My other hope is that the hacker knows it would be unwise to override the locks the way he took out the PA system, and realizes keeping confused and frantic kids in the classrooms would be in the hostiles' favor.

I have a moment of woulda-shoulda-coulda when I think of the hacker, who is clearly still in league with Marchuk's terror cell: if I'd been a more experienced operative, a better hacker, had not been sidetracked by Katie, this would not be happening. I'd have caught the target by now and we'd both be long gone from Carlisle, me at Langley and him in prison. My schoolmates would be trying not to sleep through sixth period like any other Monday.

But I only wallow in that for a minute before I get my ass in gear. I don't know how the hostiles are reacting to my announcement, but I'm going to assume the two in my chem class are still there. No doubt one of the other two, Andrews or Marchuk, is on their way back to the office for me since I broadcast my exact location. Probably not the smartest move, but it served its purpose. Most of the school should be safe inside their classrooms for now, Dodson has confirmation that her doubts about the "police" and their lockdown plan are legit, and hopefully I've shot the hostiles' Plan B to hell.

Unless they came ready with a Plan C, they'll be winging it, just like me.

I start my escape from the office a little too fast because I run smack into Jonesy's desk and jostle everything on it, knocking over his pencil cup and water bottle. Reflexively, I stand both back upright, and that's when I hear it—a dial tone coming from the phone receiver. So the phreak didn't kill the landlines in the office. Maybe he thought taking out the office lines too soon would raise suspicion in Dodson or her staff. Now that they know I'm onto them, these lines are probably next to go.

I dial 9-1-1. A few seconds later, a voice connects on the other end.

"9-1-1. What's your emergency?"

I hear a jangling sound in the hallway, growing closer.

"Hello? What is your—"

Much as I hate to do it, I hang up on the 9-1-1 dispatcher and dive under Jonesy's desk. Without knowing whether

they're hostile or friendly, I can't give away my location.
The jangling grows closer. I hold my breath, waiting for the
sound to grow fainter as it continues down the hall, but it
doesn't. It stops right outside the service window.

Please don't let it be a hostile. And if it is, please let
them think that after my stunt on the PA system, I wouldn't
be stupid enough to hang around waiting for them to find
me here, even if I actually was. At least I straightened everything on the desk above my head. Hopefully whoever it is
won't notice the water that spilled onto the touchscreen of
Jonesy's sign-in tablet.

"What are you doing here?" asks a man's voice from
outside the window.

I'm looking around the office for anything I could use as
a weapon when I hear another voice, this time female and
young. Probably a freshman; sophomore, max. A giggly one.

"Looking for Prettyboy. He's sooo cute, don't you
think?"

I used to think that was an asset until that stalker girl
made me an assassin's target.

"I wouldn't know. But didn't you hear what he just said
over the PA?"

"Trust me, he is," the girl explains, gushing, and I'm a
little embarrassed. "I was just coming from my locker when
I heard his announcement. I was hoping for a picture with
him."

"If what he said is true, do you really think he'd still be
hanging around waiting for the bad guys to come for him?"

Yeah, good question.

"So he isn't here, then?" the girl asks, her voice giving
away no fear of the school's status that I just risked my life

announcing, or of the man questioning her, which gives me hope that he's a friendly.

"Do you see anyone in there? Why aren't you in your classroom? You should get back there before your teacher goes batshit because you're missing."

So he's clearly not a Carlisle teacher. Even under these conditions, the teacher handbook expressly prohibits use of words like *batshit* with students. Maybe he's part of non-teaching staff.

"Not a problem," the girl says brightly, making me think she doesn't understand what *hit man* means. "See? I have a hall pass. And besides, my teacher—"

"Go!" the man barks, clearly reaching his breaking point with my latest fan.

I hear her footsteps moving quickly down the hall, but the man is still standing there. I hear him breathing.

To calm my nerves, I focus on the fact that my call to 9-1-1 went through. The dispatcher asked for my emergency twice. Even though I didn't respond, she has to send an officer anyway. That's protocol for all dropped 9-1-1 calls. And since I used a landline, they'll know my exact location. Help is coming. I just have to stay alive long enough for it to get here.

I wait for what seems like forever, but whoever it is must not have noticed anything amiss on the desk, must have assumed I got out of here the minute the PA system went dead, because instead of coming into the office to check it out, he and his keychain move down the hall, the jangling sound growing fainter.

I stay under the desk, waiting, keeping an eye on the clock on the opposite wall. Boulder is big enough to have a decent-sized police department but small enough that zone coverage is excellent and response times are short, especially on a hang-up call from a school. Three minutes have already passed, which means a unit should be here in another couple. I hold myself together by thinking out what I know so far so I can relay it quickly to the responding officer.

Four hostiles, most likely armed, though I've yet to see a weapon. But I must assume they are, and only keeping weapons under wraps to avoid scaring everyone. Of course, Andrews-the-Fake is probably carrying a sidearm because not having one would scare people who think she's really a cop. The bank robbers' alleged motive: hiding out in a hostage-rich environment. True motive: Ukrainian arms dealer, here to kill me as revenge for his father's death.

The clock says we're just past the four-minute mark. The responding officer should be close now. When he arrives, he'll see the metal doors over the main entrance, in the middle of the school day, and know something is wrong. He'll call for backup.

Okay, what else do I know about this incursion? Oh yeah. The hacker.

He's somehow blocking cell signals all over the building. Taking out the landlines is easy—just get to the building's network interface device and cut the phone service wire. But unless he disabled the cell tower up the road—and I know he didn't do that because the cell carrier would know immediately and that isn't the kind of attention the hostiles want—he has to be doing it from inside the school.

The clock says we're at the five-minute mark.

Wait. What if the phreak is not just blocking GPS signals but radio frequencies, too? The responding officer won't be able to call for backup. He'll have to leave to get help. That could take another eight minutes round-trip. Six if he's running hot with lights and siren. Even once he gets back here with half the department, with the hacker in control of Carlisle's security system, how long will it take for them to get inside? They'll need to bring in some heavy battering equipment or the best hacker in town.

Maybe I can't risk hiding here and waiting for help. The best hacker in town is already here.

If I can get to a computer, I may be able to figure out exactly how the phreak's blocking the signal and stop it so the police can get inside fast. If I'm quick, I might even be able to get comms up before the responding officer has to drive all the way back into town to request help. Turning off the PA system means the hacker is probably still somewhere in the school, online. After my announcement, he's probably taking down the school's entire network, in case people actually believed me. I have to get to the library's computer bank before he completes his task.

I run to the end of the hall and make a right, heading for stairs that lead to the back of the library, but as I do, I hear the familiar jangling of a ring heavy with keys coming from the janitor's supply room. So that *was* a friendly outside the office—the janitor/undercover security guard. And unless there's another person with him, he somehow has a phone that works, because he's talking to someone. But at Langley they taught me to trust pretty much no one, so I stand outside the door and listen before I approach.

The first thing I hear tells me that was a good idea: it's

the sound of leather against skin. My guess is he's slapping a blackjack—a steel paddle wrapped in cowhide—against the palm of his hand. Okay, I'm pretty sure this guy didn't find *that* in the supply closet.

"He left the office before I could get there, but the idiot kid just announced he's in the building. No one's getting out, so it's just a matter of finding him. It's a big building for only five hundred students, but not so big I won't find him pretty quickly."

Oh, dayuum. I recognize the voice—it *is* the janitor, but he isn't a friendly. Add one more to the hostile head count.

Silence on his end while someone on the other end talks, and then, "I realize he's a trained operative, but he's just a kid, so he'll be easy to take down—"

He must be talking to Marchuk.

More silence, before he says, "Yes, of course. I won't underestimate . . . right. But if he proves elusive, the girl will help us find him."

Um, what girl?

The guy laughs. "He may be an operative, but he's also a seventeen-year-old kid—all hormones. She can mess with his head. She already threw him off his game."

He's quiet, then more laughter.

"Oh yeah. He's an easy mark. The kid is just like the rest of us when it comes to foreign chicks."

I feel like I've been hit in the chest by the janitor's blackjack. Twice. Katie is working for the other side.

CIGA, J 5269

Wednesday, April 28, 2021

CHAPTER 11

As I run for the stairwell, the only thing that keeps my feet moving is self-preservation. Once there, I have to lean against the wall to steady myself. I can't believe I was wrong about Katie. I had her checked out and everything, but I guess the people she's working for created one helluva cover for her. And if I missed the mark on Katie, what else have I gotten wrong? Well, there's the janitor. I was so busy looking at students new to Carlisle, I didn't even consider new employees. The janitor and grounds-keeper were both hired at the beginning of the school year. If one is a bad guy, then I'll have to assume both of them are. That takes the hostiles' count to a definite five, and a probable six. And those last two are both former military.

Maybe that should have been a red flag, but I'd read it as a plus—they'd fought the good fight, and now they were bringing all that skill and knowledge to protect Carlisle. I never thought they'd use it against me. Now that I think of it, I never confirmed their service with Langley. It was so obvious—to me, anyway—through their mannerisms that they were ex-military, I never thought to check it out.

I'm sure I'm right about their service, but I have no idea whether it was to this country. For that matter, mercenaries turn against their own countries all the time. If they didn't, a whole section of the CIA would be out of a job.

As jacked as my assessment of Katie has been, there is one person in Carlisle I'm certain I can trust. Luckily, it's his study hall period and I know he happens to be in the library, along with a bunch of computers, working on a paper due tomorrow. Or he was until all this happened. There probably isn't a single kid in the building worried about it being midterms week right now.

I begin putting together a plan as I head up the stairs leading to the back of the library. Trying to get in through the front entrance won't work. Carlisle's library is smaller than the smallest city branch in town, so there's a better chance of a hostile seeing me. And because the entire front wall of the library is made of glass, any kids I see in there will see me too, and my arrival will be sure to cause chaos. Since there's no way I'm getting inside the library without causing a little disruption, I go for the smallest amount possible.

I knock on the door that leads from the stairwell into the back of the library—three quick knocks, pause, two more knocks, pause, and then one final knock. It's a code Bunker came up with to signify "need cover," something he planned for us to use on the wall between our bedrooms to help each other sneak out of the Morrisons' house before spending the night away with a girl. So far, there's been no need for either of us to use the code, so I have to hope Bunker remembers it.

Just as I expected—the moment Bunker opens the door, a piercing alarm sounds until I pull it shut.

"Quick, run back up to the desk and make up a reason for the alarm going off and come back," I tell Bunk, who thankfully doesn't ask any questions before racing through the stacks.

The alarm starts up a chorus of screams from the front of the library. Fortunately, the building has great insulation, because if the janitor heard the noise it would be a pretty good lead on where I'm hiding out. I just hope he's still downstairs in one of the other corridors. Soon the screams end. I hear a murmur of voices, mostly an indecipherable hum, though a few words come through loud and clear: *Loser. Idiot.*

Poor Bunker.

A minute later he returns, a little out of breath.

"I told them I was back here studying and accidentally fell against the door handle."

"And they believed that?" Seriously, lying really isn't Bunker's strong suit.

"They were happy to believe any explanation that didn't involve hit men invading the library. But I don't have much time. Ms. Larabee asked everyone to sit at the front. I told her I just needed to come get my stuff."

"Good thinking."

Bunker begins packing up his stuff but stops, a huge grin spreading across his face.

"What?" I ask.

"Can I just say—I KNEW IT!"

"Shhh. You're going to give away my position."

"I knew it," Bunker says again, this time in a loud whisper. "I knew you weren't just mild-mannered Peter Smith. And after I heard your announcement, I knew you'd come to that door to find me. I mean, if you made it. I was really hoping no one would kill you first."

"Yeah, glad I could oblige. But I'm not home free yet, and the bad guys have me outnumbered at least five to one."

"Now it's five to two. Well, more like five to one and a half, since my fighting skills are limited to the Xbox variety, but I got your back."

As scared as I am, and as little faith as I have right now in Bunker's ability to fight off a cold, much less trained operatives, I have never been so glad to have his help. When you're an outnumbered spy without a team, communications, or weapons, the situation is pretty bleak. But a real friend who has got your six can go a long way toward giving you hope.

"So what's the plan? What do you need from me?"

"I can't go into details now, not enough time, but you were pretty dead on about me—mostly."

Bunker looks incredulous, as though maybe he hadn't really believed his own theory this whole time. Then he starts grinning again, and I know I have to stop him before he starts asking me a million questions.

"I need a computer, but they're all along the front wall of the library."

"There's one back here, but it only takes you to the catalog system."

"Not if you're me." Finally, something I can do better than Marchuk and his team, including his black hat. "Go up front, let Larabee see you so she won't stress out, then see if you can sneak back here again in a few minutes."

"Won't have to. I have these," Bunker says, pulling two ancient flip phones from his backpack. They probably weigh a pound each.

"You know they've blocked cell reception, right?" I ask, but I'm not so certain they'd work even if we *had* reception. They look like something out of one of those old movies Bunker watched a thousand times in his father's fallout shelter.

"That's what convinced everyone you were probably telling the truth. They all pulled out their phones and no one could get a signal," Bunker says. "These may look like phones, but don't really work like phones. More like walkie-talkies. Two-way radios. My dad invented them."

I take one from him and look it over, skeptical. They don't look much like phones to me. "And they actually work?"

"Hellz yeah, they work," Bunker says, sounding like the same place these phones must have come from—the 1990s. "And on an ultra-high frequency band so we can communicate from anywhere in the building, even through steel walls. No Wi-Fi means they're unhackable. We just have to hope the bad guys aren't also using two-way radios and we inadvertently use the same channel. Seems highly unlikely, though."

"And you carry these around in your backpack because . . ."

"Because I always knew you were an undercover agent and I always hoped something like this would happen," Bunker says, looking immediately apologetic. "I mean, not like this, with people trying to kill you and all. You know what I mean."

"I know, Bunk. And no one's getting killed. I was able to tell the police what happened. Well, sort of. The main thing is, they know we're in trouble, but they might be a minute getting here unless I can get that computer to work. We just have to keep me and everyone else safe until the cavalry comes. You'd better get going. I'll see what I can do with that catalog system and call you in a few minutes with my status."

"I'll set the phone to vibrate, and I may have to whisper, depending on who's around. You can also leave a message, in case I can't answer," Bunker says, his voice full of nerves, as he jams the last of his stuff into his backpack. He turns toward the stacks, but stops. "Hey, what's your real name? I promise I won't tell anyone."

"I trust you, Bunk. You're the *only* person in this building I trust. It's Jake Morrow."

"Jake. *Jake*," he says, like he's trying it on for size. "I just wanted to know because, well, in case—"

I cut him off because I won't be able to stop the bad guys if I'm thinking I'll never take Bunker to his first NBA game, or eat another plate of Mrs. Morrison's chicken and dumplings, or the million other things I want to do in the next eighty years.

"In case nothing. Don't even think about it."

"All right. From now on, you're Jake Morrow to me. I mean, as long as no one else is around. I'm not going to blow your cover. I don't want to be the reason you get killed."

"I'm not getting killed. We're getting out of this, Bunker. Both of us. *All* of us."

Bunker smiles and then heads for the front of the library, probably a lot more confident in my words than I am.

CHAPTER 12

The catalog computer is in the perfect location. It's near the emergency door. I can see anyone coming, and it's in the very back of the library so no one can hear me, as long as they all stay up front. Assuming he's still logged into the school's system, I only need a few minutes to figure out how the hacker, how *Katie*—ugh, I can barely form the thought—is connected to the outside world, and piggyback onto whatever pipe *she's* using.

I haven't been working two minutes when I feel the phone vibrate.

"So how's it going?" Bunker whispers.

"You've only been gone a second. There hasn't been enough time for me to do anything yet. Can you give me a couple more minutes and call me back?"

"Oh," he says, and then nothing else.

"Bunker, you still there?" I ask, worried he's been caught using the phone.

"Yeah. It's just . . ."

"Spit it out, man. I'm kinda busy over here," I tell him, searching the school's system for the hard drive the hacker's using to control the building's operations.

"Well, I was thinking . . . all those years I spent in a hole. I finally come out and discover the awesomeness of ice cream and fireworks and girls. Especially girls." He pauses for a second, then adds, "Actually, I kinda met one already."

"And I'm just now hearing about it?"

"At first, I thought she only talked to me to ask about you. I mean, that's usually how it goes."

"You make it sound like girls are just lining up to get information on me, and yet I've never heard about it."

"Okay, it only happened a couple of times. Maybe three times. But I figured between Katie and Darlene, you had your hands full, so I forgot to mention it. They all seemed nice, but one of the girls . . . well, it turned out she was really interested in *me*."

I stop entering DOS commands long enough to finally get what he's not saying. "Instead of me, you mean. Bunker, I'd never block you, man. Never. Tell me about her."

"Not much to tell. We only talked a couple of times. But I'm telling you now because, well, who knows . . ."

Bunker's voice trails off at the end and goes quiet, and now I get it. He's as afraid as I am.

"When we get out of here, we'll find *me* a girl since you're already covered, ask them out for ice cream, and take them to a fireworks show. We might have to wait a few months until New Year's for that last thing, though."

Bunker laughs a little at that, and I realize I can work and talk at the same time. It isn't a big deal for Bunk to stay on the line with me. Actually, it makes me feel a bit calmer, doing something normal, when right now life is anything but.

"You already have a girl—two if you count Darlene," Bunker says, unknowingly crushing me. "Wait. Darlene in Texas isn't real, is she?"

"Nope."

"I knew it."

"You figured out a lot of things, Bunk." He's probably grinning at that.

"Like how I know you aren't really over Katie. What if someone tells the bad guys how you feel about her? People are afraid. They do stupid stuff when they're afraid. That would put her in a dangerous spot."

"Katie . . . well, we may have both gotten that one wrong. *Waaay* wrong," I say, not wanting to say the words out loud, but needing to, so I can make them real. "Look, Bunker, the whole reason I'm at Carlisle is because I tracked a hacker to the school. I thought this person was looking to steal defense intelligence from the local fed agencies, but now I know my target is helping these guys take revenge on me for something I didn't even do."

"And you think this person might be Katie? No way."

"I don't want to believe it, either, but I have some information that—" I stop mid-sentence, unable to tell him what I overheard about Katie because it's still too much. "Anyway, the local cops will never believe a seventeen-year-old was sent by the CIA to hunt another kid looking to harm the US government, especially since that isn't *exactly* accurate. My boss sent me to Carlisle to grow up, but now I need to reach her ASAP and tell her I was right, the terrorist hacker really is at Carlisle, but my cover and the mission have been compromised."

Bunker is silent for a second and I'm worried he's been

caught talking on the phone, but then he says, "Wow. I'm torn between being piss-myself scared right now and truly in awe."

"Yeah, well, try to avoid the first thing and definitely don't be the second one. You and everyone else could be in trouble right along with me. I messed up, Bunk."

"Hey, you just promised we'd be taking actual girls to see fireworks, so just focus on getting us out of this," Bunker says. "I'll be quiet and let you work, but maybe I'll just stay on the line while you do."

I concentrate on my work, glad for Bunker's wheezy breathing on the other end, which seems to calm me, though I can't get Katie out of my head. As much as I don't want to believe it, looking back, there were so many red flags. I was just too into her to see them. Some signs, like the fact that she's a genius in electrical engineering or that she blows away even the best guy in Carlisle's judo club, don't automatically mean someone's a terrorist hacker. I know some guys wouldn't expect those skills from a girl, but they've never met the kickass women working for the Company.

But I can't ignore recent developments, like what the pretend-janitor said about the girl with a fake accent making an easy mark out of me. Or where the hell she went during the fire drill. Did she fall back, hide in the bathroom or something, so she could be the last one out—so she could prop open the main door with the matchbook? I want so much to run all this by Bunker, but now my paranoia has kicked in.

Maybe they've planted listening devices in the library, or all over the building. If Katie really is the hacker, I can't let her know I'm onto her. And if she isn't, Bunker is right. I can't risk the hostiles knowing any more about what she means to me than they already do. I really hope she isn't the hacker, that she's in sixth-period English Lit, safe behind bolted doors. Is it crazy that I'm hoping she's okay—even if she *is* the hacker?

The wheezing on the other end suddenly stops. I hear a thud, a woman's voice, then nothing at all.

CHAPTER 13

When the phone vibrates, I'm almost afraid to answer. I'm relieved when I hear Bunk's whisper on the other end.

"What the hell happened?" I ask.

"I got caught—" He pauses and my heart damn near stops. "By a cop. Well, not really caught. She didn't see me on the phone. I was able to hide it before she saw. I know she's police, but in every spy movie I've ever seen, the agent is wise to trust no one."

I will never tease Bunker about his ancient movie collection again. "You did the right thing, Bunk. She isn't the real deal."

"She flashed a real-enough-looking badge. Ms. Larabee bought it, anyway."

"Yeah, well, she's one of the bad guys. What did she say?"

"Claimed she was doing a sweep of the building, looking for suspects, but I'm guessing she was looking for you if she's not a real cop. She left when Larabee told her everyone was accounted for."

"She even polices like a fake. A real officer would have

swept the place anyway, in case Larabee had been forced to lie."

"Exactly what I thought," Bunker says, and I believe him. He's about as paranoid as I am now. "So you really believe Katie is working with these people?"

"I don't want to, but it makes sense. To me, at least. But I can't focus on that right now. I got bigger problems."

"Can I help?"

"Well, first I need to keep everyone safe until the *real* police arrive. Next, I need to take down Kat—" I stop mid-word. Calling her by name only makes the mission harder. "I have to figure out how the hacker blocked our phones so I can make contact with my boss at the CIA, because Marchuk will soon be a national security issue again—I mean, once he's done killing me, of course. So if you can help me with *any* of that, please tell me your plan."

I don't mean to snap at Bunker. I know he's just trying to help, and that I actually came here looking for it, but I'm beginning to freak out a little. Spelling it all out like that shows me just how impossible this whole thing is.

"Sorry Bunk, I'm just a little tense. You can help me by keeping everyone up front so I can work."

"Roger that. Anything else I should know about the bad guys? Other fake police to watch out for?"

"Might be. At my last count, there are five, maybe six hostiles in the building. Which reminds me—you know the janitor who's built like The Rock? Don't trust him, either."

"Jeez. He's one, too?"

"Yeah, and probably that groundskeeper who's always out back, bench-pressing that railroad tie during his breaks,"

I say, *hoping* there are only five hostiles, maybe six. "He's small and wiry but could probably out-lift you. And they're both ex-military, so . . . no joke."

Bunker starts to say something but gets interrupted.

"Yeah, those guys are friends. That's probably who Red is talking to right now," says a guy's voice on Bunker's end. "I think he's lying about why the alarm went off. Let's check it out."

The line drops right after I hear a scream, though it may have been more like a squeal. A few seconds later, I'm face-to-face with a small search party, Bunker bringing up the rear.

"I'm sorry, Peter. I should have been paying more attention, but they snuck up on me."

"Oh my God. I sit two rows over from him in calculus," says a girl at the front of the group. "How did I not notice how hot he is?"

"Who could tell? I mean, how does *that*," says another girl, pointing to me, "compare to *this*?" She holds her phone at arm's length, presumably comparing my stalker shot to the real thing and finding reality lacking.

"No, don't you see? Just remove the glasses, take off his shirt, and boom. Hot."

I'm beginning to feel like a zoo animal, both on display and caged at the same time. Calc girl makes a move toward me, and I'm afraid she's about to demonstrate her theory, when the guy who led them all back here intercedes.

"Are you crazy? He's the reason for all of this. Stop talking about him like he stepped out of a poster on your bedroom wall."

"Peter's a good guy," Bunker says, trying to defend me, but they ignore him.

"Excuse you, but I'm into *real* art. I'm not a *freshman*," says the second girl, like it's a crime for a senior to have a Tupac concert poster on his wall. Or a couple of them.

I try to gain some control over the conversation. "Okay, wait a minute, y'all—"

"He *would* make a good poster," says the second girl. "I mean, the shirtless version. Whoever took this picture has serious skills. I wonder which filter she used, because—"

"Would you please *shut up* about what he looks like?" says the guy who is the worst nightmare of a spy who's been made: jumpy and scared. "He's probably a criminal. Because of him, we might all be killed."

"There is no way a guy that good-looking hangs out with terrorists," calc girl offers in my defense.

But her friend isn't convinced. "Not true. Remember that felon who went viral because he was so gorgeous, and then got a modeling contract after he got out of jail? And *he* had a teardrop tattoo. This one even looks a little like him."

They're all working my last nerve, and I'm about ready to stop seeing them as classmates I need to protect and more like obstacles I need to knock out of my way.

"What does that tattoo mean, anyway?" asks calc girl. "I heard—"

"Focus, people. The guy is obviously bad news," yells the self-appointed leader of the group. The three quiet ones in back nod in agreement. "Even so, we can take him. There are more of us. You two go get reinforcements. And find that cop. We'll keep an eye on him."

Bunker steps up beside me in a show of force. The whole thing is starting to feel way too *Lord of the Flies* for my comfort. As much as I don't want to hurt a student, I'm about to shut down this Jack-runs-the-island wannabe when the PA alert sounds.

I can feel the collective tension of everyone in the library rise at the same time.

"It's true! What Prettyboy says is true!"

It's Dodson, and she's clearly given up trying to sound calm. Her frantic words are followed by indecipherable noises, the screech of feedback on the PA system, and then a now-familiar voice.

"Pupils of Carlisle Academy," begins Marchuk, no longer trying to tone down his thick Ukrainian accent, *"what headmaster is trying to tell you is, school has been taken over by me."*

There is a murmur of voices at the front of the library, and probably all over the school, as people try to digest this information.

"We are here for only one reason. We are here for person you know as Peter Smith." He stops for a second, and there is muffled conversation on his end before he resumes. *"Or perhaps you know him as Prettyboy. Sooner we find him, sooner we leave. You can help—"*

He's stops talking and begins moaning like someone is killing him. Then we hear a thud, followed by his voice sounding far away: *"Вона брикатися мене!"* which translates to *"She kicked me!"*

It doesn't take a genius to figure out where, considering all the moaning. Score one for Dodson.

There are some indecipherable sounds on the other end,

more squealing feedback from the PA system, and then Dodson's voice, sounding way past frantic.

"Don't believe him! They won't just leave. We must pro-tect Prettyboy for all our sakes, because the minute they find him, they'll—"

The next sound through the PA system is clear, at least to me: the sound of a fist hitting bone. Dodson's down. A second later, the only thing I hear are the screams inside the library, including the one coming from my mob's leader, who runs off toward the front of the library.

"Just as I suspected," I say. "He's the type who only jumps bad until the shit hits the fan."

"Uh, he's the type who will turn you in to the bad guys to save himself," calc girl offers. "He was talking about doing that even before Dodson's announcement."

Next thing I know, Bunker takes off after him, but not before yelling back to me, "Keep working! Find a way to get help."

I'm worried whether Bunker might have taken on more than he can handle, but he's right, and so is Dodson. Even if a mob hands me over—or I do it myself—Marchuk isn't just going to walk away from this. Dodson and her people have seen his face. I remember what he said in that shelled-out house back in Ukraine. He'll use kids as human shields if that's required to make his escape. Turning myself in will save many more lives than we'll lose, but that isn't a cost-risk assessment I'm willing to concede. Not yet. I don't plan on losing a single person.

"We aren't going to stop you," calc girl says as she puts up her hands and looks around at what remains of the mob, who nod in agreement. "Do what you gotta, Pretty-boy."

She turns to leave and the group follows their new leader.

I know the police are on their way, but it's taking too long. Maybe they're having trouble breaching the security doors. I need a backup plan, and getting CIA-grade help might be the only thing that saves us, so I get to work, hoping Bunker can deal with whatever's happening up front.

Come on, Jake, you can do this. You've stopped hackers from taking down Wall Street.

First, I need to figure out whether the hacker is block-ing communication by spoofing radio frequencies or jamming GPS signals. He—or she—would need some mad skills to pull off the first thing, skills I probably can't match, so I'm hoping it's the signal jamming. I'd have a chance against that.

No, man. Either way, you got this. The reason you're only seventeen but work for the best spy shop in the world is because you've hacked into the Defense Intelligence Agency just for kicks.

Okay, I am *this* close to locating the system partition the hacker is working behind. Once I find it, he—or she—is toast.

Yeah, but when you breached the DIA, your life wasn't on the line then. Worse, you weren't the reason a whole school's worth of people are on lockdown.

Al. Most. There. Aha! Found you, phreak. I'm coming for you now. You can't hide from the great Jake Mor—

And then the system crashes. That ain't good.

A second later, the walkie-talkie phone vibrates.

"Bunk?"

"Yeah. It's chaos up here."

"What did you do to that guy?"

"Well, right now I'm sitting on him, because he's threatening to escape the library and turn you in. But after Dodson's announcement, I think the rest of them are on your side. Any luck with the hacking thing?"

"Uh . . . I think the hacker knows what I'm up to, which means he—*she*—probably knows my location in the school. I have to get out of here," I say, scanning the walls and ceiling of the library for an air vent.

"I'm coming with you."

"Don't think so, Bunker. I'm going through the air shaft."

"Tell me where you're going and I'll get there."

"Ms. Flagler's bio classroom. I can drop through the vent there to reach the supply room," I say, grateful I memorized the building's blueprints before I even landed at the Denver airport. "There's an old desktop."

"But you said the phone was dead in there."

"I don't think the hacker took down connectivity wholesale; she's just taking off-line any PC she thinks I might access."

Saying the words and naming Katie as the culprit sounds so wrong, like saying Lois turned on Clark and joined forces with Lex Luther, but I can't deny what's happening.

"Doesn't that include the supply-room computer?" Bunk asks.

"That PC has a phone line plugged into the wall," I explain as I drag the table closer to the nearest vent. "It uses dial-up on a separate dedicated landline, and it's so infrequently used I'm hoping she doesn't even know about it."

"I won't ask you to explain all that, but I *am* coming with you."

"That computer is a long shot, but it's the only shot I have. It's a risk you don't need to take, so just—"

"No, sir. I'm not going to just hang out in the relative safety of this library and let my first best friend also be my last. I'll get there. I'll find you, and then—"

And then the line goes dead.

CHAPTER 14

I pull my Swiss Army knife from my backpack before climbing onto the table and removing the screws holding the vent to the wall. Once inside the air shaft, it's easier to move through than I expected. The ducts are wider than I thought, and look brand new. Air-shaft-crawling was part of the syllabus in my Breach and Incursion class at trade-craft school. The ducts we practiced in were the usual flimsy sheet-metal type that buckle and groan as you move through them. Thanks to Carlisle standards requiring state-of-the-art everything, these ducts are not only wider than most, but they're made of a heavier stainless steel, allowing me to move through them noiselessly.

It doesn't take long before I'm in the shaft above my chem class. Through slats in the air vent, I can see down into the room where my classmates are still being held by the hostiles. Only one is within my view. But I can't slow down to determine whether the second one is still in there, so I continue on toward Ms. Flagler's bio classroom, which is when I hear voices on a radio. It only takes a few seconds of chatter before I recognize the radio is tuned to a police band. The hostiles must be listening in, trying to see if their location has been made by the cops.

"Unit thirty-one, please check in with a status on Carlisle Academy."

The kids in the room below let out a collective sigh, but no one is more relieved to have heard those words than I am. It's confirmation that my 9-1-1 call lasted long enough to register as a hang-up call and for the system to give my location, forcing the PD to roll a unit to check on us. Yay for landlines. Bunker is right. Sometimes old-school is better.

But my relief is short-lived.

"Thirty-one. Carlisle is an all clear," says a voice I recognize as fake-cop Andrews. I can only imagine what she's done to the real Unit 31. "Just a kid high on something, so messed up he threatened to prank us again if he isn't allowed to skip an exam."

"No additional unit needed, then?" asks the dispatcher.

"Affirmative. I'll wrap this up soon, get the parents in here to deal with him or drop him at the ARC if he gives me a problem."

"Roger that, thirty-one."

The ARC is the Addiction Recovery Center in our town—what police departments used to call the "drunk tank" in the old days. Unless these hostiles did one helluva reconnaissance mission before they arrived, there's no way they should know that level of detail about the local police. I only know about it because Duncan The Douche landed there a few weekends ago and was stupid enough to brag about it, trying to show me how gangster he is.

So there's a reason she sounded so much like a cop when I first heard her in the office—a reason the police-band dispatcher didn't question whether Andrews was impersonating the officer known as Unit 31.

Andrews *is* a cop. A dirty one.

Directly below me, I hear someone say, "We're screwed."

"Notice how he got away right before this happened, like he knew it was coming and didn't even warn us?"

I know that voice, even if it's only a loud whisper. Duncan.

"You heard Dodson," says the other guy. "It's good he got away. Maybe he's trying to get help."

"Yeah, you keep believing that. I'll be over here working on an actual plan."

One of the hostiles yells, "Shut up back there! No talking."

This is just what I need—The Douche going rogue, but not before inciting a riot in chem class. Maybe I was right to include him on my suspect list. Maybe I should have been looking for more than one. Could Duncan be in on it with Katie? *Nah, Jake, that's the paranoia talking.* Duncan is just being Duncan. But one thing I can agree with him on—I need to handle business myself because there is no cavalry coming.

When I start moving toward the next classroom, the hem of my pants snags on the pointy edge of a screw in the vent, pulling on the metal panel just slightly before it releases. My heart starts racing a mile a minute while I pray no one heard it. But that small noise was enough. I hear a male voice say, "Go check it out. I'll stay here to watch over our backup plan out of this place."

This remark starts my classmates talking, which makes the lead hostile freak out and start yelling at everyone to "shut the hell up or else," which only encourages the talking to turn into shouting and screaming, providing cover for me to move through the shaft, past the ventless supply room, until I am over Ms. Flagler's room.

The vent gives me the perfect vantage point to the classroom's door. Just as I'd expected, one of the gunmen arrives, peering through the window. He must see what I see—an empty room—because he leaves after unsuccessfully trying the knob, apparently satisfied.

But I'm not. He hasn't studied the school's security system schematics the way I have. The lockdown from individual rooms can only be initiated from the inside. Someone is inside the room, hidden from the hostile's view and mine.

I have no choice. I have to get to that supply-room computer, but I'm hoping whoever's down there is a friendly.

I drop into the room, knowing I'm completely vulnerable to attack. My heart nearly stops beating when I hear a squeaking noise the minute my feet hit the floor. But it isn't a human. It's a complaint from a pack of guinea pigs I almost crushed. They've somehow escaped their cages, running all around the room. I think I know why the bad guy was satisfied with what he saw. Hopefully he figured one of the pigs had gotten into the walls or the air shaft, that it wasn't a human who'd made the noise that caused his partner to lose his shit.

I just about do the same thing when I hear a noise. It's the turning of a doorknob, but not the one the hostile just tried to open. It's coming from behind me. I scan Ms.

Flagler's classroom in search of a weapon. The closest thing is a stool at one of the lab tables, which is a joke of a weapon if this guy is armed.

The door to the supply room slowly creaks open. His actions are deliberate. Fearful. Whoever it is probably isn't armed either, which means I have a fighting chance. All I can do is turn around, get into a defensive stance, and hope I'm right. Or better yet, hope it's a friendly coming through that door.

CHAPTER 15

Oh, thank God. They don't come any friendlier. It's Bunker emerging from the supply room, and he's dragging Mr. Maitland with him.

"Found him hiding out in there," Bunker says in a near whisper. "Says he was on the way from his class to the office when you made your announcement, so he ducked inside. Fortunately, he didn't have the wits about him to lock down the room until after I arrived."

"You got here?" I say, mostly ignoring his Maitland story. It's more of a statement than a question.

Bunker smiles. "Told you I would. Had to cut you off because the *real* loser in the library was giving me a hard time. But the rest of the kids took over for me so I could come help you. They're on your side. Besides, this whole thing will make for a great story when I ask out my future girlfriend."

Bunker is talking about this girl, and all I want to know is how he made it here in one piece. "But how?"

"Just took the stairs and the hallway. You were right. There can't be many bad guys running around. Didn't see a single one on my way here."

I don't even try to hide my astonishment. Bunker pretends he doesn't notice it and continues on, sounding like it's just a regular day at ol' Carlisle Academy.

"I released the pigs for cover."

"Great idea, Bunker. It worked."

"And I already checked out that PC. The hacker must have guessed you were headed here next, because it's down, too. But Maitland here is going to let us borrow his laptop. He claims he can still get a connection."

That is strange if it's true. Why leave Maitland with access? But I hope he's right. "Hand it over," I say.

"No," Maitland says, holding the computer in a death grip against his chest with both arms. "I need it so I can receive—"

I throw a left hook across his face and knock him the hell out. Not only don't I care what he needed the laptop for, I'm pissed he's in here hiding out instead of heading back to his class and trying to keep them calm like I'm sure every other teacher is doing right now. Plus, I just can't stand the guy and will probably never get this chance again. I did it for national security, not to mention Carlisle. At least he had Bunker there to catch his fall, because I wouldn't have.

"Better hide him in case a bad guy checks the room again," Bunker says as he drags Maitland to the corner.

Out of sight of the door's window, I open Maitland's laptop, close out the classroom roster he had up, and bring up a DOS screen.

"Now, let's see if he really is connected. I was this close to finding where and how the hacker is jamming our signals."

My hope-o-meter goes from zero to sixty and back to zero in under ten seconds.

"Should have known I wouldn't catch a break like that. If Maitland had a connection, he doesn't now."

The hacker probably detected Maitland's usage and shut him down. I try looking in the laptop's disk cache in case there's at least a clue that might help me track her down.

Bunker comes over and stands behind me. That usually drives me insane, but I'm thinking, after the day I've had so far, I'm going to be a lot more chill about stuff like that.

"One day you have to show me how to do some of this stuff," Bunker says. "I just don't get how a bunch of zeroes and ones can shut down every phone in the building. I mean, how is that even possible?"

I stop typing for a second and let his words sink in.

"Bunk, you're a genius."

"I am?"

"I don't think she's spoofing. The whole reason I was ever in U—" Gah, I'm so excited to figure this out that I almost blabbed about my Ukraine mission. "Um, earlier this year, the hacker did a thing that put the two of us on a collision course."

"What *thing*?"

"That's classified. But trust me, she screwed up big time, which means she probably doesn't have the skill to spoof. She has to be using a jammer."

"How does all that make me a genius?"

"Your average pocket-sized cell phone jammer has a range of maybe eighty feet. But this school is huge, with high-grade construction and very thick walls."

"And so . . . ?"

As I talk it through, I feel my heart race like it did when I was in the air shaft over chem lab, but in a good way this time. I know I'm onto something.

"Everywhere I've gone in the building—the exits, hallways, stairwells on all three floors—I could never raise a cell signal on my phone. Not only that, I heard the janitor talking on his phone. That can only be possible if the hacker is using one seriously hard-core jammer, one with an external antenna that can be tuned to individual frequencies."

Bunker shakes his head like he's trying to clear water from his ears. "Dude. You're talking gibberish."

It makes so much sense to me now, and I'm so relieved to finally take a step forward instead of two steps back that I'm talking so fast Bunker probably wouldn't understand me even if he had a clue about zeroes and ones.

"A jammer like that needs its own electric source and would be very noticeable inside the building. She's on the roof. Or at least her white noise generator is. The signal jamming is too effective to be coming from anything else or anywhere else. We need to get up there and take out that noise generator."

"Okay, let's do it," Bunker says, already heading for the door.

"Slow your roll. With those two hostiles next door, we can't risk taking the hallway. We don't have time to escape through the air shaft," I say, already working on a plan. "Help me carry Maitland back in sight of the door."

Once that's done, I pull the expandable baton from my

backpack, unlock the door, then stand on one side of it, out of view. Bunker gets the idea, grabs the metal coat rack from behind Ms. Flagler's desk, and takes up guard on the other side of the door.

"Now we just need to get their attention."

I grab a textbook from a bookshelf, open the door, and throw it at the lockers across the hall before closing the door and getting back into place.

We aren't in position for ten seconds when we hear someone trying the doorknob. And just as I'd hoped, when the hostile enters, there is a brief moment between him seeing Maitland on the floor and realizing someone else must be in the room.

That's when I land the steel baton against his pterion, the weakest point on the skull, immediately incapacitating him.

Or possibly killing him.

That's a step in my development as a covert operative I'd hoped never to take. I never expected I'd have to, despite all the scenarios the Company psychologists tried to prepare me for. It calms my stomach a little when I place two fingers against his neck and find he still has a strong pulse. He'll probably live long enough to die of something else. Hopefully while in a supermax prison.

I motion to Bunker, and he immediately drags the body out of sight of the window while I close the door, leaving it unlocked. Maitland remains in position, bait for the hostile's partner, who will surely arrive at any moment.

The problem I'll face with Hostile #2 is that he'll be more on guard. Not only does he know I'm in here, he'll suspect I've taken out his partner. He'll be angry about leaving the classroom, which means leaving his hostages— and his safe passage off the campus—unattended. He'll be worried the hostages won't believe whatever story he told to keep them from leaving the classroom. His adrenaline will be pumping just a little harder. He'll be a little afraid. He'll be far less predictable than the first guy.

I take my position beside the door again. When Bunker moves to take the same position he held for the first hostile, I raise my hand, signaling him to stay near our latest unconscious captive. Bunker gets it. He knows I want him to make sure the captive stays that way. I'll have to deal with the next guy on my own. With my back pressed against the wall, I can feel the vibration of the door in the next room opening, then closing again. I nod at Bunker. The second hostile is coming.

As soon as he hits the doorway, and before he can put one foot in the room, I slam the baton into the man's stomach.

The plan was for me to knock the wind out of him so I could easily get him into a choke hold. But dude didn't get the memo. When the wand hits his stomach, it's as though I've struck metal, and the energy of the strike reverberates through my hand.

For a brief moment, the sensation causes me to loosen my grip on the baton, allowing the man to take it from me with one hand and aim his sidearm at me with the other. He smiles, but there is nothing in his eyes but cold, hard murder.

"Doesn't Marchuk want me alive?" I ask.

"Yes. But I don't care what Marchuk wants."

You know how they say your life flashes before you when you're about to die? It doesn't happen like that for me, not like a movie, anyway. Right now, I'm thinking it was good Rogers made me that offer, and I'm glad I said yes, even if it's about to get me killed. She gave me something when I'd given up on having anything. I'm thinking I've already gone out with a really dope girl and maybe it's okay that I'll never know for sure whether she was one of the bad guys. And I'm feeling so afraid, so desperate for something to hold on to even as I'm on my way out, that I try to remember my parents' faces and, for the first time since forever, they come to me as clearly as the last time I saw them.

He raises the gun and points it at my heart.

This is it. He's taking me out.

Suddenly he just crumples to the floor as though his legs have been cut out from under him.

Bunker has thrust the bottom end of the coat rack, fencing-style, into the back of the hostile's knees. It incapacitates him just long enough for me to come back to this world and apply the choke hold I'd planned before he came *this* close to killing me.

I admit I'm more than a little pissed-off about that, about what he almost took from me, so once again, this guy is very lucky Bunker's here. No one has spent hours preparing Bunk for all the emotion and potential crazy that comes from seeing the life leave a man by your own hands, and it would probably scar him for life.

It doesn't take more than a few seconds for me to

compress his carotid artery and jugular vein to the point where he's out cold, but—thanks to Bunk—still breathing. Otherwise, I may have applied the hold a few seconds too long, and then he wouldn't be.

CHAPTER 16

Bunker and I quickly strip the two hostiles of their clothes. The set I change into reeks of cigarettes and sweat, but I don't have a choice. Being dressed like them will help us if we're caught making our way to the roof. Or at least we hope so. Bunker is about eight inches shorter than the shortest of the two bad guys, and the clothes fit him that way. The shortest guy was pretty ripped, but on Bunker, his shirt is much too tight and his pants half a foot too long. If we run into the janitor, fooling him into thinking we're his fellow bad guys may not prove as successful as we hope. At least we'll be wearing their Kevlar vests, which explains why it felt like I hit metal when I slammed my baton into that second hostile's chest.

We've changed into full combat gear—everything but the masks—and are about to look for something to tie up our quarry with when we hear footsteps behind us, coming from the supply room and sounding way too heavy to belong to a guinea pig.

"What the hell?"

I turn around, prepared to fight yet another hostile,

and for the first time since ever, I'm relieved to see Duncan. I think.

"Jesus H. Christ—are those the terrorists?"

"Technically arms dealers to terrorists, but yeah," I confirm, but offer no more. Duncan seems to be a little in shock, not that I can blame him after the way he's spent the last thirty minutes.

Duncan stares at me like I'm a riddle to solve, then asks, "Who the hell are you?"

"Clearly not who you thought I was," I say as I circle the room, ripping the cords off every electrical appliance I can find and throwing them to Bunker.

"Clearly."

"And who are you?" I ask, stopping long enough to watch his reaction.

Duncan looks genuinely confused. "What are you talking about?"

"I'm asking if you're friend or foe. Last I heard, you suspected I escaped the room just in time to save myself but not the rest of you."

"How do you even know about that?" Duncan asks as he starts giving himself a pat-down, probably looking for a bug. Despite the crazy that is happening all around us, watching The Douche have a near breakdown is fucking hilarious. Bunker is busy hog-tying one of the hostiles, but I can hear him snickering.

"Like I said—I'm not your average Carlislian," I say, trying hard not to laugh so I can mess with his mind just a little more. "So how's that escape plan you were working on?"

Duncan starts patting down his lower half and stops when he hits his pockets.

"Here. You can have your five dollars back."

I start tying up the other hostile but not before snatching my money from him, because hey, the Company has me on a tight budget, and I'm hoping I'll live another day to use that money.

"Why are you here, Douche?" Bunker says, apparently feeling himself now that he's been made my unofficial partner. Duncan doesn't say a thing about it, either.

"When they didn't come back, I had to check it out," Duncan explains.

"That was either very stupid of you or very brave."

"Well, after sitting in class for the last half hour wondering whether we were going to die, somebody had to see if there was a chance to run."

I come this close to taking back my comment about him being possibly very stupid, and telling him how cool it was of him to take that chance, but I just can't do it. He's still Duncan. But maybe now I'll stop thinking of him as The Douche, at least.

"All this time I've been hassling you, this is what you could have done to me?" Duncan asks, looking around the room. "You took these guys out with . . . with what? I don't suppose you're packing heat at school."

"No one's been 'packing heat' since the nineties," Bunker says as he hog-ties Bad Guy #1 with an extra-long extension cord. "Even I know that. He did it mostly with his bare hands. And I helped."

I look at Bunk as if to say, *Stop talking,* but it probably doesn't matter anymore. What little was left of my cover is long gone, thanks to my stalker making me an internet sensation. Besides, I can tell Duncan's emotions when he found us were real. He can't be the hacker, probably isn't working with her, and he definitely isn't a gorgeous British girl.

"Look, Duncan, I don't have time to explain. There are more of these guys on the loose and they're hunting me down."

"But why? Who *are* you?"

I stay quiet for a second as I secure the hands of Bad Guy #2 with a handcuff knot, thinking of how to explain.

"Let's just say I work for the government."

Duncan lets that sink in for a second. He looks astonished, or sick to his stomach, I'm not sure which. Then he says, "Are you saying you're a—"

"I'm saying I have to bounce. Now. The school is locked down, we can't get out, but I may have a way to contact the outside and get us some help. But there are more where these two came from, at least four more, and when these guys can't be raised on their radios, one of their friends will come to check. So we have to move."

"We? Does he 'work for the government,' too?" Duncan asks, nodding toward Bunker while making air quotes.

"Yes," I say, cutting Bunker off before he can explain himself. We don't have time, and I've decided after he had my six with that coat rack, he deserves to be deputized.

"I want to help," Duncan says, shocking me for the second time today. "Let me come with you."

"You can help by keeping an eye on our captives. They should be out for thirty minutes to an hour, but you can make sure they stay that way," I say, handing him my baton. "Use it if they come to."

"I can do that." Duncan looks down at the hostiles before he notices the third man slumped against the wall. "Is that another one?"

"No, that's Maitland," Bunker says.

"World-Geo Maitland?" Duncan asks, going for a closer look. "Wow. He's one of them?"

"No. At least, I don't think so. He was just collateral damage. Don't worry. He's still alive," I say.

Duncan half smiles and asks, "You're sure?"

Yeah, pretty much no one likes Maitland. For a guy who hasn't been at the school a whole semester yet, he's already made a ton of enemies.

"Before you start watch on these guys, go back and let the chem lab know what's up. Wait—is everyone okay in there?"

"Sure. Physically, anyway. They're holding up."

"Good. The main thing is to keep the rooms locked from the inside. As long as everyone stays in the rooms, they'll be okay. And don't trust anyone you don't know," I say, wincing as I think of Katie. "And be suspicious of people you do. The janitor and the groundskeeper—"

"The ones who look like they spend the whole day at the gym?"

"Right. They aren't legit. Neither are the two who have Dodson, even though one of them is actually a cop."

"Yeah, I know about them," Duncan says. "We heard them on their radios. The real cop is Andrews, the fake cop is Marchuk, and there's another one called Koval."

"Koval must be the janitor," I say, the name sounding

vaguely familiar. "Stupid of them to use their names over the radio, though."

"I think these two aren't the brightest of the bunch. The one called Koval kept yelling at them every time they used his name. He must be in charge."

"Marchuk's in charge, but Koval must be his second-in-command. Good looking out. That's useful information," I tell him, surprised to find saying something nice to Duncan isn't as painful as I'd have thought. I guess being held hostage is a good way to make friends out of foes. And the way Duncan is cheesing, you'd think I was the agency director himself paying the compliment.

"Speaking of staying informed," Bunker says, reaching into his backpack. "In case things start going south in here . . ."

Duncan looks as confused by Bunker's ancient brick of a phone as I was. And how many of those does he carry around, anyway?

Bunker tells Duncan, "It looks like a phone—"

"Not really," Duncan says.

Bunker ignores Duncan's assessment and continues, "But works like a walkie-talkie. You'll be able to contact Peter and me with these."

Duncan takes the phone, looking doubtful.

"Bunker, leave your hostile's radio too, so Duncan will know if one of the others is coming."

Bunk and I put on the ski masks and head for the door.

"Hey, Smith," Duncan says.

"What?"

"How is this thing really going to go? What's going to happen to us all?"

I'm thinking this thing is going to go badly, but Duncan doesn't really want to know that. He wants to believe we'll all be safe in our beds tonight trying to forget this day ever happened.

"These guys like to work below the radar. They're taking a chance just being in this country. No way will they compromise themselves any more than they already have by hurting anyone but me."

Duncan doesn't look convinced. "If you really believed that, if you truly think you are the only person they'd hurt, wouldn't you just give yourself up so the rest of us can go free?"

When I don't answer, Duncan continues, "That's okay, Smith. Dodson clearly doesn't believe it, either. Since they've locked us all in here, looks like we're in it with you. Do you really think you'll get us out of this?"

"Yes," I say, hoping I sound more certain about it than I feel. I want to tell him that I'll die trying, but I figure he doesn't really need to know that extra detail. "Lock the door behind us."

CHAPTER 17

The minute we step out of the room, I hear a faint but familiar tinkling sound coming from the other end of the hall, and I don't even have to guess who it is. The janitor, aka Koval. That's when I remember why his name seemed so familiar the first time I heard Duncan say it. He owned the voice I didn't recognize back in Ukraine during the shootout, the voice that suggested Marchuk kill me then. I hand Bunker my backpack and whisper to him to run for the stairwell and wait for me. He hesitates for a second—I'm not sure whether he's afraid for himself or for me, but I'm guessing both—then follows my command.

Not only don't I want Bunker to be the one caught, but there's no way he'll fool the hostiles that he's one of them.

I quickly pat down the pockets of my cargo pants, and find cigarettes along with a book of matches that looks just like the one I found jammed in the front door when this became the worst day ever. By the time Koval turns the corner, I'm leaning against the chem lab door, a lit cigarette in hand, and hoping in the thirty seconds it will take him to reach me that I'll come up with a plan. He surprises me by stopping at the end of the hall.

The radio on my shoulder squawks.

"What the hell are you guys doing down there? You were supposed to check in five minutes ago."

He talks as though he's from the Midwest, maybe. Anywhere, USA. Considering his Ukrainian name and that he works for Marchuk, I'm guessing he's affecting the accent non-Americans go for when trying to speak our English. Which means the guy I'm impersonating is probably an actual American. A traitorous one.

"Needed a break," I say in my best New York accent, waving the cigarette in the air as proof. "Fucking kids getting on my nerves."

"What about Owens—did he need a break, too? Because he didn't check in, either."

"He's inside."

"That's where you should be," Koval says. It sounds more like a threat than an order.

"Right. Just let me finish this one up."

Even from this distance, I hear him let out an exasperated sigh. "Check in every quarter hour. Don't make me have to come down there next time. We can do the job with five just as well as we can do it with six," he warns, before going back the way he came.

I crush the cigarette under my foot and run for the stairs, hoping that from this far down the hall, the click of the stairwell door shutting sounds the same as the chem lab door.

I find Bunker just inside the slightly cracked door, looking scared and pissing me off a little.

"Oh man. You should have gone out for the drama club. I thought we were done for."

"We might have been. If Koval had come down the hall, he'd have noticed this door wasn't fully closed."

Bunker looks confused. "I just wanted to hear what was going on, to make sure you were okay. It was barely open."

"Guys like that—like *me*—we're trained to notice things most people don't. What you think is just a little thing slightly out of place kicks us into threat-assessment mode. Depending on how threatened we feel, we neutralize the threat first, ask questions later."

I hate to call him out at a time like this, but if Bunker's going to play operative, he has to do it right or he'll get us both killed.

"Got it, chief," Bunker says without a hint of sarcasm, and I know that's the last time I'll need to teach that lesson. "So now what?"

"I still need to contact my boss, so now we head for the roof," I say, taking the steps two at a time. Surprisingly, Bunker is keeping up. "It has to be where the hacker is hiding out."

"You still think it's Katie, huh?" Bunker asks, beginning to sound winded after running four flights.

"I've run the data, Bunk. There's no one else it could be."

Neither of us says anything the rest of the way upstairs. Bunker is out of breath, and I don't want to discuss the possibility that the first girl I've ever really fallen for might be trying to kill me.

When we reach the door to the roof, I start calculating the risks of opening the emergency exit, sounding the alarm, and luring out the three bad guys still inside the building. There's always the possibility the hacker has locked this one down too, but I doubt it. It's the only way back into the building, and in the event she needs to move quickly, the roll-down door would slow her escape by at least thirty seconds.

"She could be using a satellite phone. Maybe I can use my phone to try hacking her internet connection and call my boss."

But first, I set the timer on my watch for eleven minutes.

"What's that about?"

"Remember what the janitor said? If we don't check in on the quarter hour, he'll come looking for us. We caught a break being in the hall where we could hear him and his keychain."

"I can't believe Dodson hired a terrorist," Bunker says.

"I'm sure she can't either," I say, "On the plus side, I confirmed the hostile count. Six. Koval's the only one who can walk the halls without raising suspicion. Two are with Dodson and the office staff, unless Andrews is still on the prowl looking for me. I figure the groundskeeper was given outside duty in case someone managed to call the police. As long as he stays outside they're down to three inside, now that we've taken out the two in chem lab."

"Assuming Duncan can keep them that way."

"He'll be fine. He's got a ruthless streak."

"I hope you're right. I don't really want to die today."

"You aren't going to die today," I say, hoping it's true.

"Especially not after I finally found the girl of my dreams."

I look up from my phone and shake my head at him.

"I've had a *lot* of dreams about girls, so I know. Dreams are all you have when you spend your first fifteen years underground without ever seeing a real live one."

"If she's on a sat phone, I'm not having much luck tapping into it," I say, though I suspect Bunker is so into telling me about his crush that he's forgotten why we're here.

"She smells like flowers and has hair like Daryl Hannah in *Splash*."

"Like who in what?"

"The movie?" he says, as though that explains everything.

"Yeah, never heard of it."

"It's one of my dad's favorites. Daryl was my first crush. Anyway, my girl's hair is blond and long and wavy. Kinda wild, like she's spent the day on the beach, except without the tan."

No matter what I try, I can't get into Katie's sat connection.

But trying to break into it makes me recall something about Maitland's laptop when I first opened it back in the bio classroom. The last thing Maitland looked at was his fifth-period roster. He should have had sixth period open, not fifth, which ended before lunch. Now that I think about it, if he really did have connectivity, shouldn't he have been trying to call for help, not studying his class list?

"She's nothing like Katie. I guess you and I have different tastes," Bunker continues. "Well, not *that* different. Isn't it funny how we both found girls with English accents? Though I'm not certain my girl is English. Maybe Scottish; she has a little brogue thing going. It's adorable."

I've been so busy trying to crack Katie's connection

and wondering about Maitland's part in any of this, I mostly tuned out Bunker as he went on and on about his crush, but this last thing gets my Spidey sense tingling.

"Oh, should I shut up? Am I keeping you from concentrating on the hackery?"

Just then, we're interrupted by the PA system alert, followed by the voice of Pavlo Marchuk.

"Prettyboy, I'm tired of these games. I have something you want. If you ever want to see her again—alive, that is— you will be in main office within five minutes. Otherwise, you will only want her in your dreams. Or should I say, nightmares?

"Five minutes, Prettyboy."

Marchuk just did my risk assessment for me. I shove my phone into my pocket and go for the emergency door.

CHAPTER 18

Out on the roof, from the vantage point of the door, there is no one up here but us. All I see is freedom, miles of mountains and blue sky, but no way to reach it.

"What are you doing?" Bunker shouts over the screeching of the emergency alarm.

I pull the mostly full pack of cigarettes from my pocket and stick it between the door and the jamb. "Keeping us from being locked out."

"No, I mean, shouldn't you be going to the office? Now you have proof—not only that Katie isn't the hacker, but that the bad guys have her."

"That isn't proof she isn't one of them." I've learned it's better—easier—to expect the worst than to be sucker punched by it. "For all I know, Marchuk's announcement is a trap and he doesn't really have her."

"If it was *my* girl, I wouldn't take that chance."

When Bunker was going on about his romance a minute ago, I was too busy trying to hack Katie's phone line to really hear what he was saying, but now his words come together like a Rubik's cube.

"Your girl. You said she smells like flowers. Let me guess—roses and honeysuckle?"

"Um, I have no idea. But I guess she might. Those are flowers."

"You said she asked questions about me. What kind of questions?"

"Basic stuff. But she was just trying to start a conversation, using *you* to get to me for a change."

"It isn't Katie!" I say that way too loudly, but I can't help myself. *It isn't Katie.*

"I tried to tell you."

I'm so relieved, but I don't have the heart to tell Bunker this time's no different; this girl was like the others, using him to get to me.

"So shouldn't you be rescuing her instead of hanging out on the roof?"

I look at my watch. "I still have four minutes. Your mermaid—does she have crazy-long, flaming-red fingernails?"

"So you know her!" Bunker says, smiling so big I almost hate to break it to him. "The nails are hot, right?"

"What they are is a great disguise. No one expects talons like that on someone who spends most of her waking hours on a keyboard." Then I recall the suggestion she mouthed to me as we stood in the fire drill line. "I should have known that girl wasn't a freshman."

"What are you talking about?" Bunker asks.

"Don't you see it?"

"See what?"

"The girl you're dreaming will be your future baby mama

is the same one who started the whole 'prettyboy' thing on Twitter—an attempt to throw me off my game, I think. A successful attempt, obviously."

Bunker just stares at me blankly.

"You know what that makes her, right?"

I can tell from his expression that Bunker's finally starting to get it. The guy is usually a brainiac, but like Koval said, accents can make even the smartest man stupid sometimes, even when they're fake, and especially when they come with a pretty face and mermaid hair. More like Medusa hair than a mermaid's, now that I know who she really is.

"No way," he says, incredulous. "You said it was Katie."

"Oh, so *now* you believe it could be Katie?"

"I do when you're suggesting the love of my life is a terrorist hacker."

"Well, if she's somewhere up here with a satellite phone and an internet connection, she'll prove me right," I say, moving toward the four huge HVAC units, the only place on the roof to hide.

As we approach, I check my watch—just over three minutes left on the clock—and the pockets of my borrowed cargo pants for a potential weapon. Blondie may be the size of a pixie, but she may be as well-trained as I am.

Bunker watches me release the safety on the blade of the folding knife I found and asks, "Are you crazy? What if you're wrong?"

"Trust me. I'm not."

Sure enough, there she is, sitting on a milk crate behind the first HVAC unit we check, still wearing my Clark Kent glasses and smiling like she still thinks this is all one big game. Bunker, on the other hand, looks like he's about to be sick. She waves at him as though she has no clue she's just ripped out his heart and stomped all over it.

"Hey there, Bunker," she says with an English accent.

Bunker says nothing.

"Let me see your hands," I yell at her.

"I'm not armed. Marchuk would never allow that. He'd worry I'd come after him."

"Why would you do that if you're working for him?" I ask.

"Only against my will."

"You expect me to believe that?" I ask as I grab the computer off her lap.

"I don't care what you believe. It's the truth. He forced me to manage the school's security system so he could grab you. It was only supposed to be about you—no lockdown, no one else in danger—just take you out of your chemistry class and go. But you weren't there. If anyone's to blame for the mess it's become, it's you."

"Maybe she's right." When Bunker finally speaks, I don't like what he has to say, especially when I only have two and a half minutes to reach Katie. "Maybe we should listen—"

"I don't have time to listen," I say, handing the knife to Bunker. "Stand up."

I'm surprised when she does as I order, but unlike Bunk, I'm not trusting her they-made-me-do-it story, especially since her accent has slowly morphed into a mix of BBC and something I can't pinpoint, maybe Eastern European. I skip the formality of asking her permission before I pat her down, looking for weapons.

"Where's your phone?" I ask after finding no weapons on her.

"What phone?"

"I know you've got a satellite phone up here some-where."

The minute I step back from her, she reaches down the front of her shirt—the one place I was too much of a gentleman to check—pulls out the smallest sat phone I've ever seen, and throws it over my head, a good fifty feet behind me, and off the roof. I hear the tiny splash it makes when it hits the koi pond in the courtyard. Okay, seventy feet.

"Oh, you meant *that* phone."

Wow. She's a pretty decent hacker who actually does look like Hollywood's version of a mermaid *and* has an arm like an MLB pitcher. I can see why Bunker might lose his damn mind after only two conversations with her—if she wasn't a terrorist bent on seeing me dead.

"Sorry, but if Marchuk found out I gave you access to the outside world, he'd kill me," she says. "You'll have to get us out of this without my help."

"There is no 'us' here. You're one of the bad guys. We aren't. Right, Bunk?"

He doesn't say anything.

"Bunk?"

"Yeah?"

"Are you going to be okay?" I ask, not sure I'll believe his answer either way. But I don't have a choice. Katie needs me. "Blondie here needs to be contained, but I have to get down to the office. Like, stat."

"You really do. You're under two minutes now, and Marchuk's threats are never idle. I should know." The way she says that last line and looks at me with pleading eyes is probably meant to convince us she's a victim in all this, but I'm not buying it.

I'm not so sure about Bunker.

He finally wakes from the dead and says, "Yes, I can handle it. But not with this. I don't want that."

I take the knife but trade him the small canister of pepper spray I found in one of my pockets. Bunker waves it off.

"Look at her, Peter. She's barely five feet and weighs, like, ninety pounds."

"But you can't—"

"Let my guard down, I know. I figured you out, didn't I?"

"You're sure, Bunk?" I ask, hoping he is, because now that I know Katie isn't the hacker, she's back to being the first girl I ever really cared about. I'm now under ninety seconds.

"Yeah, man. I got this. You go help Katie."

"No fireworks and ice cream, right? And definitely no mermaids."

"What's he talking about?" Blondie asks.

"No mermaids," Bunker says, taking the pepper spray to prove he means it.

I don't quite believe he's "got this," but I have to leave him with the hacker. Katie is waiting for me.

When I reach the office, so out of breath my chest hurts, Officer Andrews is holding Katie by one arm, or more like holding her up. Her beautiful face is already bruised and swollen, her bottom lip cut and bleeding, no doubt from the fist Marchuk landed on it. He's sitting at Jonesy's desk, feet propped up on it, looking like he rules the world.

"Here is Prettyboy, with only seven seconds to spare. You cut it close. Perhaps Marchuk was wrong and you don't care for girl as much as I was told."

I want so much to feel my hands around his neck that I have to keep myself from charging into the room before I've assessed every threat it holds.

"What kind of man hits a defenseless woman? Your father would be so proud. If he were still alive, I mean." I know those are fighting words, but I want nothing more right now than to reunite him with Marchuk Sr.

"So, girl *is* important to you. Good. You will make less trouble for us this way, I am certain."

"Let her go, Marchuk. No more games. If you've come for me, I'm right here."

"Like most seventeen-year-old children, you are under impression world revolves around you. How is it you work for CIA? Why do they let boy do man's work? This would never happen in Ukraine's SBU."

"I got your boy right here," I say, clicking open the knife Bunker refused to take.

"Don't. She's got me," Katie says. Whimpers, more like, which nearly makes me lose my shit.

But I don't. Andrews's holster is empty and I can guess what she's jabbing into Katie's back. The only reason Katie's in this office is because she means something to me.

I throw the knife onto the desk.

Marchuk takes the blade and holds it on me while Andrews ties me to a chair. Ugh. Wherever he's been hiding out all this time, he still hasn't stopped eating borscht three meals a day, or discovered antiperspirant.

"Don't worry, little one."

He walks up close to Katie and strokes the side of her face he hasn't turned an ugly shade of purple. She looks so afraid it's damn near killing me.

"Such pretty girl. Pavlo appreciates that you agree not to fight. Pavlo will take good care of you, at least until he does not need you."

If thoughts could kill, he'd be so very dead right now. I search his eyes for any bit of his father in them. Marchuk Sr. was a bad person who did bad things, but he still had some humanity in him—I know that better than anyone. In his son, I see the same facial features, same brown hair and eyes, same complexion—dark, considering he's a white Slavic dude. But any humanity? There is none. It's like looking into the eyes of the man who would have killed me if not for Bunker.

Marchuk is going to kill me, even if he takes his sweet time doing it. And then he's going to kill Katie, but not before doing something awful to her first. On instinct I jump up, lifting the heavy office chair with me, but Andrews has my arms bound tight. I guess Marchuk is worried I have Bruce Banner–like rage because he hauls off and lands a right cross that feels like a sledgehammer against my face.

I actually see stars before the chair and I fall back to earth.

CHAPTER 19

When I come to, only Katie and I are in the office. She's sitting on the edge of a desk, watching me while dabbing her eyes with a tissue. It makes me wanna-kill-him angry at Marchuk all over again.

"How long was I out? Where are they?"

"A couple of minutes. They're in Dodson's office, plotting something, I suppose." She tosses the tissue in the wastebasket before wagging three fingers in my face. "How many?"

"Six."

I thought the situation could use a little levity, but I guess not because Katie looks worried. I try to smile, but it hurts like hell.

"Three. I see three fingers."

"You bugger," she says, but I can tell she's more relieved than mad.

"They left you unsecured? Why didn't you run?"

"Run where?" she asks, amazingly composed considering she must have been bawling a minute ago. Her eyes are red and her lashes are still wet. "The school is locked down. That will only anger him."

The door to Dodson's office clicks open. I let my head drop to my chest as though I'm still passed out. A moment passes before I hear the door click shut again.

"All clear," Katie says after a few seconds. "Andrews was just checking whether you were still unconscious. Or maybe she's concerned you're dead."

"Don't worry. They can't take me out that easily."

Katie takes a seat at the registrar's desk, picks up a mirror she finds there, and checks out her face before looking over at mine. "I'm just glad she was the one who worked me over instead of Marchuk. For your information, this is what happened the last time I tried to run."

"I'm here now," I say in my best it's-all-under-control voice. "I'm going to get you out of this."

"Oh, really? I'm not the one mildly concussed and tied to a chair right now."

She has a point. And I also notice for the first time that she's not in Carlisle's uniform. Except for the shoes, she's wearing the same gear I am: black long-sleeved t-shirt, black cargo pants.

"Why are you dressed like that?" I ask.

"Oh, this old thing? I took them off a bad guy. He didn't need them anymore and in these situations, they're far more comfortable than a skirt and blazer."

Now it's Katie's turn to bring some comic relief. I know she's trying to put on a brave front for me, but I still wish I knew why Marchuk made her dress like that. Given that last comment of his before he knocked me out, maybe I don't want to know. Dude is clearly a freak.

"Why are you?" she asks.

"Why am I what?"

"Why are *you* dressed like that? I assume it has something to do with that little spectacle you made on the PA a while ago."

Odds are good we're going to die no matter how bad-ass I'm pretending to be for Katie's sake. I want her to know Jake Morrow before that happens. So I'm about to answer with the truth, but before I can, Marchuk and Andrews come out of Dodson's office.

"You are in land of living again," Marchuk says to me.

"And you're here, in the land of the free. How is that possible?"

Marchuk ignores my question. "Enjoy living while you can. It won't be for much longer."

Katie sniffles, and when I look over at her, she's crying again. She must be so scared, going from dry-eyed to waterworks in under ten seconds.

"Do not worry, little one. You will have bit more time. My promise to you." He smiles all nasty before barking an order. "Now move other chair over there, next to boyfriend, and have seat. Andrews, go check on office staff in auditorium."

Katie drags her chair next to mine and takes a seat, but Andrews doesn't move, only says, "They're locked down. They aren't going anywhere."

"And they are tied up too, but I still want you to make sure all is well. People working in school must be smart. People escape. I should know."

"Maybe we should get Koval to handle that."

"Koval is busy keeping other men in line. And making sure hundreds of soft targets stay where they should be. And also making sure package is secure until *other* package arrives safely. So, no, I do not want Koval to do all these jobs and your job, too. I want you to do what I tell you to do."

I'm making mental notes of Marchuk's cryptic talk of "packages" in case I live long enough to decipher them, but I'm also preparing for him to explode. If he does, it would be the right time to strike, if I can figure out how to do that without the use of my hands or feet. Unfortunately for her, Andrews doesn't seem to notice Marchuk's about to go ballistic on her.

"But don't you need me here to—"

"What—help with boy tied to chair? Or with sweet girl?"

"But this kid, isn't he some kind of agent?" Andrews says, which makes Katie turn to me and ask, *You're a what?* with her eyebrows. At least, that's what I think she's saying. Eyebrows are hard to read.

He slams his fist on the nearest desk, shattering the thick glass that was meant to protect the wood beneath it. Okay, Junior is really strong.

"I think Marchuk can handle situation. Do as instructed."

"Yes, sir," Andrews says.

"But first, if team two is even three seconds late with next check-in, please kill them. No, wait. We can't afford to lose two men. We already have one who has not reported in. Only kill one of them. To make point."

"Which one?"

Marchuk throws his hands in the air and looks at Andrews as though she asked him for the answer to world peace. "Does not matter which one. Just do it."

I assume team two is still tied up and unconscious in

Ms. Flagler's bio lab, which means Duncan's a sitting duck. The digital clock on the wall facing me reads *01:44:17.* I don't know how I'm possibly going to get Duncan out of this jam in forty-three seconds, but I have to try.

"Team two is probably on a smoke break," I say, before Andrews can leave the office. "One of them is a chain-smoker."

"How do you know this? Team two says you were not in classroom when they arrived. But perhaps you returned and made sure they would not be able to check in. It would explain your clothes."

01:44:39

Oh man. Marchuk just read me like a book. I hope he can't also read the panic I'm feeling right now. *Play it cool, Jake.*

"You think I don't keep fatigues in my locker for just such an occasion? And I've been moving all over this building since 'they arrived' and I saw one of them taking a smoke break, more than once, even if he didn't see me."

01:44:52

"I think you would be happy having us down to four, no? Why do you care so much about this?" Marchuk asks.

I don't have an answer for him.

01:44:57

Andrews's radio comes to life. A heavy New York accent says, "All quiet on the western front."

Oh no. That means the hostiles must have come to. I never liked Duncan, but I also never wanted this for him. I can only hope they gave him some of what Katie and I got, and stopped at that.

"Ah, so he will live another day. Just as well. Really could not afford to lose one more, but my anger gets best of me and Marchuk does not always think straight," he says, adding a chuckle as though he's talking among friends, before he yells at Andrews to go do what she was told.

I'm trying to figure out which man is down. Obviously, the two in the chem lab are awake. Hold on a minute. That punch must have really messed me up. They can't be, or they'd have already told Marchuk about what Bunker and I did, unless they were too afraid to let Marchuk know they'd been taken down by two high-school kids. Even if they left that part out, wouldn't they have at least warned them there were two of us on the loose? For all they know, Bunker's a CIA operative, too.

"Now, let's get to business, shall we? You killed my father. This makes me very angry."

I've just seen his "angry." Don't need any more of that, so I try to diffuse it.

"I didn't kill your father."

"Your people did. I was loading truck, saw whole thing from across compound. Father raised his weapon first. He meant to take offensive." Marchuk pauses for a second like he's trying to collect his thoughts as he remembers that day. Maybe he isn't 100% monster. "But you were there, inside house. For some reason, he liked you. He only hesitated in firing first because of you."

He turns his back to us for a moment before whirling around again, a whole different expression on his face.

"So, now you die. Only question is how," he says, rubbing his hands together like a B-movie villain before placing a duffel bag on the desk. "Marchuk has many tools for job."

So not only am I about to die, it's going to be a horrible way to go. And if that isn't enough to think about, now I smell smoke.

"Wait, does it smell like something's burning?" I ask.

"Is that best stall tactic you have?" Marchuk asks. "CIA training is not so good as I thought."

"*CIA?*" Katie says, this time with words. "You're a CIA operative?"

"I'm serious," I say to Marchuk, ignoring her question. "I smell smoke."

Or is it tar? Whatever it is reminds me of the smell when they're paving a road. No, it smells more like a fireplace. It seems a weird thing to worry about when I'm about to be tortured, but I actually do smell smoke. In a locked-down building filled with hundreds of people. Unfortunately, neither Katie nor Marchuk seem worried about it.

"I will enjoy killing you same way you killed my father, and making girlfriend watch."

I believe it. I don't remind him that I didn't *actually* kill his father. At this point, it doesn't seem relevant, and I'm more concerned about what he has in store for Katie. I wish I could at least grab her hand, but all I can do is lean as close as I can to her. When I do, instead of strawberries and cream, I get a whiff of fireplace.

"It'll be all right, Katie, I promise. Try not to worry," I tell her. "Look, Marchuk, I'm more valuable to you alive than . . . not alive."

"You are of no value to me in any state. But why would you think so?"

"I know that hacker you hired last spring caused all your problems when she allowed me access to your client list." Marchuk doesn't say anything, but I can tell he's listening, so I keep going. "And I know for damn sure I'm better at this game. Clearly, the CIA thinks so. You'd get a twofer with me—best hack in the business, and an operative trained by the best in the world."

Marchuk paces a couple of times before he asks, "And you would turn your back on CIA? Why?"

"To save all these people. They haven't done anything to you."

"Did I say I was going to kill them? No. I said I would kill *you*. They are just incentive to keep you in line, but now I have you. You do this to save yourself," Marchuk says, all up in my face. Or more like *sprays*, and I can't even wipe my face because my hands are tied. Then he smiles and adds, "Ah, yes. You offer this to save girl too, no?"

"Does it matter why I'm offering?" I say, as tough as I can for a guy with his arms tied behind his back. "It's a good offer and you know it."

"Perhaps. But I also know you are wrong about two things. One, SBU—not CIA—is best in world." He smiles all sinister before he says the next thing. "Two, hacker may not be as good as you, but offers me much more than you can."

"Marchuk, if you—"

I don't get to finish pleading with him because he lands his fist against my jaw.

"Also, it does not matter, because you killed my father. So, on to killing. It will be bad for him, pretty girl, but

Marchuk is gentleman. Once I tire of you, your death will be quick. Don't worry."

I hear Katie sigh before she says, "I swear to God, if another man tells me not to worry—"

It's the last thing I hear before the room is suddenly filled with smoke.

CHAPTER 20

At first, I'm disoriented from the smoke and probable concussion. Then my senses are assaulted all at once: I hear the click of a switchblade springing open; I feel the sawing motion as the rope that binds me to the chair is cut; I smell tar, smoke, and just a hint of strawberries and cream. By the time I shake off the cut ropes and escape my chair, I see Katie bringing down Marchuk with a brutal kick to his junk. I hate Marchuk, but I can't help but feel for him.

At least until she hooks her foot around his ankle, sweeps his legs out from under him, then straddles his back. I'm certain it's an image I won't soon forget—girl of my dreams on top of the guy who wants to kill me.

"Uh, need some help there, Katie?"

"Yes. Hand me my purse, please. It's on that desk behind you."

That wasn't the kind of help I was offering, but since she now has both of Marchuk's arms behind him, I figure she may not need it anyway. I didn't see this playing out with Katie saving the day instead of me. She must have taken a self-defense class. From the looks of it, she must have been the best in her class there, too.

When she reaches up to take her bag, which must weigh about twenty pounds, I realize what I'd been smelling on her. Not woodsmoke and not tar, but creosote, which smells like a combination of both and is used to treat railroad ties, which is what the fake groundskeeper likes to bench-press.

"So you weren't lying when you said you took those clothes off a bad guy," I say, sounding a little stupid. More like a little stupefied. Okay—a lot stupefied.

"Maybe that concussion is worse than we thought," Katie says. "Why would I lie about something like that?"

"Okay, not lie, but I thought you were making a joke."

"Why would I make jokes at a time like this?"

"Maybe to lighten the mood?" Like right now. This mood could definitely stand some lightening. I suppose people handle stressful situations differently. I like a little humor. Katie gets more serious than death. Maybe because Marchuk is beginning to recover from the ball-kick she gave him and is starting to squirm. She still doesn't ask for my help, though.

"I mean—*how*?"

"How what?" she has the nerve to ask, at the same time she grabs Marchuk's hair and slams his face into the floor, knocking him out.

"How the clothes? How the smoke bomb? How the . . . what you just did to Marchuk there?"

"So many questions, Peter."

"Well, the clothes I figured out. They're a couple sizes

too big and smell like creosote, so I'm guessing you took them from the groundskeeper."

She sniffs her sleeve. "Really? That is one keen sense of smell you have there."

"Yeah, it's a gift. I assume that guy was outside the building acting as a lookout."

"You assumed right. At least, I think that was supposed to be his job, though I found him inside."

"Not such a great lookout if he got himself trapped inside after the building was locked down."

"I suppose. But he had that just-came-in-from-outside smell." She looks up at me and smiles. "Hey, who has the nose now?"

Why is she acting like restraining the man who was about to kill me is all in a day's work? Unless . . . it actually is.

"He *is* a groundskeeper. Maybe he always has that smell," Katie says. "Anyway, I've seen him checking me out before, so I was able to lure him into one of the stairwells, knock him unconscious, and take his clothes," she says, clearly skipping some important details, like how she could possibly knock out a guy who lifts railroad ties like they're nothing. Or where she left him, because I didn't see an unconscious groundskeeper in any stairwell.

From the bag she pulls a pencil case. I've seen it before and thought it had to be the only pencil case in all of Carlisle, as much a relic as Bunker's brick-phone walkie-talkies. I always figured it was a British thing. Katie digs around in the case like we've got time to select the perfect writing utensil, all the while sitting on top of a twitching Marchuk, until she finally selects a red fountain pen.

Except it isn't. She pulls the pen apart and reveals an already-filled hypodermic needle. She plunges it into Marchuk's neck.

"And I don't lie," she continues as though all that didn't just happen, while patiently waiting for Marchuk's twitching to stop. "Well, of course I *lie*. It's what we do, isn't it? But I didn't lie about that."

"So . . . what about the groundskeeper?"

"Oh, I just gave him a little carfentanil, zip-tied him, and dragged him into the nearest closet. That took *forever*. He's small, but all muscle."

"Carfentanil?"

She holds up the needle she just pulled from Junior's neck.

"It's ten thousand times stronger than morphine, so it acts quickly, and it only takes a drop or two. Vets use it to sedate elephants," she explains, finally getting off of the now-unconscious Marchuk. Or possibly dead Marchuk. "Which makes two down and I'm not sure how many to go, unfortunately."

"By my count there are six altogether, but four down," I say, finally glad to add something to the script. "Bunker and I took out two more. Duke Duncan's with them in the chem lab, making sure they stay that way."

Or at least I hope that was him who just checked in with Marchuk.

"Excellent! Just two more, then. We need to stay on task and complete this mission." She slings her purse—though I suspect it's more than a purse—across her body and heads toward the door. When I don't follow, she turns back to me.

"Unless you don't want to help?"

I'm still in a daze, and it doesn't have anything to do with my possible concussion or the smoke bomb Katie just happened to have on her.

"I'm trying to figure out what the hell you know about a *mission*."

She narrows her eyes at me like she's trying to decide how much she wants to tell me. Or how truthful she wants to be about it. "I may have left out a few facts when I told you about myself over dinner that one time."

"So when you said lying is 'what *we* do,' did you mean—"

"Of course that's what I meant. They have girl spies too, you know. And speaking of facts, you left out a few yourself. The CIA. My word."

"But I . . . I mean . . ."

"No time for that now. I have a job to do."

"What job?"

"Let's just say I need to make sure a package is secure."

Her answer surprises me, mostly because I didn't expect her to give me one. Yeah, it's pretty vague, but it's more than I knew about her thirty seconds ago. The fact that Marchuk said the same thing when he was listing Koval's duties means I still don't know nearly enough about Katie.

"Stay here and babysit Marchuk if you want, not that he's going anywhere anytime soon."

"Are you sure you didn't kill him? You used *elephant* tranquilizer."

"No need for that messiness. Besides, there wasn't enough tranquilizer left to kill him—I need to ration it. But he'll be down for hours, and by then, we'll have neutralized the remaining two and evacuated the school."

If you count the hacker, there are actually three remaining, but I figure I should hold back as much information as I can until I can learn as much about her mission as possible. She heard me mention the hacker, but I assume Katie has no idea she's in the building, or what her role is in this current operation.

"So you agree, those are our priorities—neutralize and evacuate—in that order?"

Katie hesitates a second too long before she agrees with me, and now that I know she's an operative, I read something into that hesitation. I store the clue for later, and actually smile when I think about solving the mystery that is Katie.

"Good. Andrews is supposed to be in the auditorium guarding the office staff, but we'll have to track down Koval."

"He could be anywhere," she suggests, sounding defeated, like we might as well not even look for him. Her response doesn't quite match the Katie I've witnessed over the last few minutes.

"Marchuk said he gave Koval three jobs: watching the other men, watching the soft targets, who should all be locked down in their classrooms, and 'making sure package is secure until *other* package arrives safely.' Koval must be somewhere working on that task. You don't think one of these packages is yours, do you?"

"Why would I?" Katie answers casually, just as a trained operative would if she were hiding something.

I know why I'm here—to track the hacker. I know why

Marchuk is here—to kill me. Or at least, I thought that was his only reason, until all his talk about the packages.

Now it seems he had another plan to execute once he finished executing me.

What I don't know is why Katie is here. She isn't going to just tell me, so my best bet is to play along until I gain her trust. Or until I have to force her to tell me.

"Hey, can't blame me for asking. So I think the first thing we need to do is make sure Duncan is okay with the two bad guys he's guarding," I say. "Do you have any more of those needles? We could give Duncan some help by drugging the hostiles."

I'm talking to her like I trust her, but the only thing I trust completely about her is that she's an agent of some government. Only an operative could calmly eat M&Ms—a handful of which she just grabbed from a bowl on the registrar's desk—while discussing how to neutralize possible Ukrainian rebels/terrorists/arms dealers.

"I told you I'm already running low," she says, "and with two more to take out, we probably should conserve it. How did you take them down in the first place?"

"With a sleeper hold."

"Well, we'll just run down there and you can put another one on them. That should tide Duncan over awhile."

Is it just wrong that it makes me all kinds of happy to hear Katie talk about applying choke holds to bad guys as though she's listing errands we need to run? Like, *Oh, and let's grab a bag of Funyuns from the 7-Eleven.* At least until I remember why I've heard of the drug she used to knock out Marchuk.

"Wait a second. Isn't carfentanil the stuff the Russian

police used back in the day, to smoke out some Chechen rebels when—"

"Someone paid attention during hostage-crisis mitigation class at Langley, I see. Want some?" she asks, holding the bowl of M&Ms out toward me before grabbing another handful for herself. "I am *so* hungry. And we just had lunch, too. Dealing with that groundskeeper really took it out of me."

She's noshing while I'm over here worried the government she works for is enemy number one. "Uh, no thanks. About the carfentanil?"

"Don't worry, Peter. I didn't use that much of the drug. And I'm not KGB."

I'm glad she didn't call it by the current name—FSB. Probably everyone but actual Russian agents still call it KGB, so that's a good sign. Still, Katie may not be Russian, but Ukraine is just next door.

She polishes off the M&Ms while I help myself to a Sharpie from Jonesy's pencil cup because I can always find a use for a Sharpie and duct tape. He had a roll of it on his desk before lunch, but now it's gone. I grab the switchblade off the desk and follow her. As we make our way toward my chem class, I remember what Koval said about the girl with all the accents. I know now that he meant the hacker, but it does raise a question.

"So is that really a British accent you're working, or just a cover?"

"It's an *English* accent."

"Same thing."

"How very American of you. *British* means I could be from Scotland, Wales, or Northern Ireland. I'd think a CIA operative would know that. And yes, my English accent is real," she says as we pause at the end of Corridor A so I can use my periscope to check around the corner. Koval may be roaming around, moving those packages Katie claims to know nothing about. She adds, "I suppose I can tell you who I work for, since you told me."

I don't mention that I didn't tell her I work for the CIA. Marchuk did. I mean, she's Katie and everything, but I wouldn't have given up that information so quickly. Well, I was going to before, but that was when I thought I was about to die.

"If you're *English*, I'm guessing you work for MI5?"

"That's our version of the FBI," she explains without missing a beat. "I work for the Secret Intelligence Service. MI6."

"I always get those two mixed up. You guys could stand to add a little creativity to your agency naming. No one's mixing up CIA and FBI," I say, but in truth, I know the difference.

I'm just glad she does, too.

"So, what's an MI6 operative doing at Carlisle?"

"You know how it works, Peter. Tit for tat. You told me who you work for, I told you, and that's all you get. Unless . . ."

"No way am I telling you why I'm here. For all I know, you still haven't told me the truth about which government you're from," I say as we reach the chem lab.

I knock lightly on the door and look through the window. For the second time today, or the second time ever, Duncan looks relieved to see me. When he comes over to unlock the door, his look of relief turns to surprise.

"Why is she with you?" he asks when he lets us in. Even under these circumstances, I can tell Duncan is miffed.

He, like practically every other guy at Carlisle, has a crush on Katie. Unlike every other guy at Carlisle, he actually had the nerve to ask her out and got rejected. It was probably the funniest of the many funny stories Katie told me on our one date. Now it makes me wonder if she's funny for real, or just as a cover.

"Oh, Peter rescued me," she says before I can respond.

She wants to keep her cover, so that was probably the hardest lie she had to tell. I'm pretty sure Katie doesn't need any rescuing, and would hate admitting it if she ever did.

"He didn't do the greatest job of it. What happened to your face?"

"Oh, but he did, and it's an amazing story. I'll have to tell everyone about it one day when we have more time, but that isn't today. Right, Peter? Tell Duke how we have to go, now that we know everything is okay in here."

"Go? Go where?" Duncan asks. "The whole time I've been terrif—*terrifically* concerned that these guys would wake up any minute."

"The way Bunk and I tied them up, they're no threat even if they come to," I tell him, but I see it's no help. Though he didn't quite admit it, I can see in his face that he really is terrified. I try to boost his confidence. "Great job on the New York accent, by the way. I was actually worried it was the hostile."

Duncan still looks "concerned." Rather than try to convince him otherwise, I kneel down next to the hostile who'd gotten the choke hold earlier and land a hard blow to his head. That gets a gasp out of Katie, who is really selling the damsel-in-distress bit. It's quite the performance, which means I shouldn't trust her farther than I can throw her. That will be hard to do when every night she's been the last thing I think about before I fall asleep, ever since the day I met her.

She hears a sound in the corner and turns to find Maitland, still tied up but conscious.

"Our World Geo teacher is one of them?" she asks.

"No, he's just collateral damage," Duncan says, mimicking what I told him earlier, I guess in an attempt to impress Katie. "But just in case, I taped his mouth when he came to. I wasn't sure if I should knock him out like Peter just did to that guy. I mean, he is our teacher, as far as we know." This last sentence sounds more like a question than a statement.

"That's right, Duncan. As far as we know," I assure him.

Though I didn't confirm it when he asked who I really am, Duncan is by now convinced I'm not just the nerd-boy he got a kick out of tormenting for the last eight weeks, and he's acting like we're now on the same team. And I guess we are. We all are, really. Everyone in the school.

"But now we have to go," Katie says, a little too urgently. Apparently she's forgotten the role she's been playing.

"Go where? You can't stay, Smith?" Duncan says, also forgetting his big-man act and sounding a little scared.

"We've— I took down two other hostiles, which I think leaves two more," I explain. "I need to find and neutralize them before we can figure out how to get out of here."

"Shouldn't Katie stay here, where it's safer?" Duncan says, turning to Katie. "Don't worry. I'll protect you."

Uh oh. He probably shouldn't have said that. I step in before Katie can go ballistic.

"Duncan, I think she'll just feel more comfortable staying with me. Isn't that right, Katie?"

Fortunately for Duncan, I'm able to keep her response limited to a serious eye-roll.

As we head for the door, Duncan says, "Wait. What about the other one? Aren't you going to punch him, too?"

"The first hit I gave that guy will keep him out for hours. Another one might kill him."

Duncan looks satisfied, or as satisfied as a kid can be whose biggest worry this morning was not failing the German midterm. He wishes us luck before he locks the door behind us.

CHAPTER 21

The second she steps into the hall, we hear a voice I recognize.

"Hey! What are you doing down there?"

"That'll be Koval," I whisper, maintaining my position in the alcove, out of sight. "When he reaches you, I'll flank him and we'll take him down."

"No," she whispers back.

"No? That's definitely him and he's getting closer," I say as his jangling keys grow louder.

"Trust me on this. I can't blow my cover yet."

"But your clothes—"

"Stay hidden. Please, Peter."

Even though she's been looking down the hall toward Koval this whole time, I'm watching her, trying to decide whether to trust my instincts or hers.

At the last second, I duck into the bathroom, leaving the door open a crack so I can hear whatever's about to go down. This would be the perfect opportunity to take Koval, even if he's armed. He won't expect two of us. But her last request was more like a plea, and by now I know Katie isn't the kind of girl who begs for anything.

There's something going on between her and Koval, though she claims to know nothing about him. I don't know what Katie is playing at, or whether I should trust her as she asked, but I stay back.

"I was in the girls' room when that announcement came on, and I've been afraid to come out. So . . . is everything still horrible out here?"

"Afraid so. We're still on lockdown."

"So why aren't you hiding somewhere?" Katie asks.

"Well, I'm not just a janitor."

Uh oh.

"Carlisle hired me as undercover security."

I knew it. Not that it matters now.

"So what are you going to do about all of this?" Katie asks accusatorily, apparently forgetting she's supposed to be playing a scared student.

"Not much I can do against a team of bank robbers, except walk the halls looking for kids like you who shouldn't be out here. Hey, why are you dressed like that?"

"I'm supposed to be in drama right now. We're doing *Evita*. I play a soldier."

Koval is quiet for a few seconds before I hear him say, "You should probably come with me."

"I'll just go back to my class now, but thanks."

"I don't think that's best," Koval says, sounding a lot sterner than he has up until now.

"Let go of me," Katie says, the last word muffled by what I suspect is Koval's hand over her mouth.

All I can hear is the sound of their feet moving down the hall, and then no sound at all.

I play all the scenarios: Koval is putting on a great act

as the loyal school employee trying to protect her; he thinks she's just a student, and therefore leverage to negotiate his way out of here; Marchuk has told him what Katie really means to me, and he's going to hurt her.

Since I'm trained to assume the worst, I choose the last scenario. With Katie so reluctant to blow her cover, she won't fight him until the situation becomes do-or-die. She'll be on the defensive, never a good position. And if she does fight, it will have to be hand-to-hand because she's left her bag here.

Katie is pretty kickass, but I don't like her odds in that situation. Koval's a big dude.

Just as I step out of the restroom, a girl comes out of the one opposite. She lets out the beginning of a scream before I can grab her and cover her mouth. It takes me asking her three times whether she can calm down before I free her.

"Oh my God, I've been looking for you and here you are!" she scream-whispers.

Even at a loud whisper, I recognize her voice. It's the way-too-perky girl who ran into Koval outside the office earlier.

"Shhh," I say, hustling her back into the girls' bathroom, which she takes the wrong way. Very wrong.

"Oooh, you want a little privacy, huh? That's fine by me, Prettyboy."

"Why are you just roaming the halls?" I ask, holding her at arm's length. Or at least trying to, since she's squirming around attempting to, I don't know, kiss me, I think. "You do understand there are terrorists running around, right?"

"Honestly, I haven't seen a single one. I think maybe

you're just putting us on. Oh my God, is this a prank? That's what it is, isn't it? I *knew* it!"

My fan makes me think of the movie Katie and I saw during our one and only date. After we left the theater, she spent ten minutes analyzing why there always has to be one in every scary movie ever made. You know the character—her silliness draws the ax murderer toward the group just as they're about to get away, and she's about to get everyone killed until someone slaps the stupid out of her? Katie insisted no one like that exists in real life, and if she did, her girl-card should be revoked.

I'll have to tell Katie I found one.

"This is not a prank, and I really don't have time for this. I have to find—"

"Promise me you'll take me to the winter dance, and *maybe* I'll believe you."

"Look, uh, what's your name?"

"Rachel."

"Rachel—do you really think Dodson, the woman who has zero sense of humor, would be in on it with me? You heard her announcement, right?"

This seems to make the girl think for a second.

"If you've been running around the school looking for me, you know everything's been locked down. Do you really think I could manage to take over the security system, like I'm some kind of genius hacker or something?"

"I suppose not."

Time to land the kill shot. "And I just watched Katie Carmichael get taken away by one of the bad guys."

"So this is for real?" says the girl, finally getting it. Only problem is, I think she may have gotten it too much. Her eyes go wide and she drops her phone. "Oh my God. What are we going to do? We're going to die, aren't we? We're all going to die!"

"Well, we are not going to freak out," I say, though it may already be too late. "We're going to stay calm and make a plan to save our homecoming queen."

Rachel is silent, just staring at me like she may have gone catatonic, but at least she isn't screaming.

"Are you still with me, Rachel?"

"Yes."

"Okay, good. We need to create a diversion. I have a lighter; we could set some paper towels on fire, maybe set off the sprinkler system. Unless she's disabled that system, too," I say, talking more to myself than to Rachel as I think through a plan, "and even if she didn't, the alarm might scare everyone into leaving their classrooms."

"Where is Katie?" Rachel asks, suddenly coming to life.

"I think she's in the janitor's office. Why?"

"Give me three minutes," she says, heading for the door, "and I'll give you one big fat distraction outside the janitor's office."

"What are you gonna do?"

"You'll see! Just get ready."

I'm scared to know what she's planning, but I need to be focused on Koval when it happens, so I don't press her for details. But I do ask her one last question before I leave.

"Which class should you be in right now?"

"Sixth-period World Geo, but don't worry, because my teacher—"

"Isn't there. I know. He's kind of tied up right now," I say, before she takes off running like she stole something.

What I don't know is why Maitland wasn't in his class when the lockdown happened, and I'm starting to think it wasn't a coincidence. But I got ninety-nine problems and Maitland is like, ninety-eight on the list.

When I reach Koval's office, I was right in guessing he'd bring Katie here. I hear her voice but I don't dare sneak a look inside, in case Koval is watching the door. Instead, I stand just outside of it, waiting for Rachel's distraction to arrive.

"Please, sir . . . *please*," Katie is pleading, "I don't know what you've been told, but you have it all wrong."

I hear a murmur of voices at the end of the hall, and turn around to see Rachel and about fifteen girls, presumably from Maitland's class. She gives the thumbs-up sign and I return it, sick to my stomach.

But I don't have much time to think about it because suddenly the hall is filled with screams and squeals of what seems like a whole lot more than fifteen girls. And they're all yelling "Prettyboy." I feel the way I do every time I board a roller coaster, a jumble of fear and happy anticipation of what's to come. But I need to be all business now, so I get my head right, act like a CIA-trained operative, and feel what I need to feel to get through this moment: nothing.

The minute Koval steps out of his office, I land my fist against the side of his head. It stuns him long enough for Katie to get out of the room, but it doesn't bring him down. It probably hurt me more than it hurt him. It feels like I've broken a phalange or two. If ever there was a candidate for horse tranquilizer, this is the one, but Katie's bag of tricks is still on the alcove floor.

It's something I never want to do to a guy, but I have to resort to Katie's and Dodson's tactic and kick him in the jewels. That brings him to his knees, but I know it won't be for long. I'm about to finish him off by landing a kick somewhere more lethal, but Katie stops me.

"Don't kill him, Peter."

That request only confirms my suspicions—Katie is working with Koval—but I don't want Katie to know I know. Besides, I'm mostly concerned about the safety of sixth-period World Geo's female population right now.

So while Koval is still down, I get behind him and apply a sleeper hold while shouting at the girls to get back to class. But of course they don't move, other than to shuffle back a few feet, and worse, Koval won't lose consciousness. I brace against the lockers for leverage, but the guy is so strong, he's able to fight the hold. All I seem to be able to do is make him groggy. I pull the folding knife from my pocket.

"No!"

"He won't go down, Katie. I have to—"

"You have to leave him alive. If you kill him before . . . before I have confirmed something . . ."

"What are you talking about? You have to give me more than that," I say, still holding on to Koval's neck. Now I feel his body going slack. The sleeper hold is finally taking effect on him, but I probably won't be able to put him under for very long. My arm is running out of strength.

Katie looks at me. No arms crossing her chest, no eye-rolling, no hands on hips. Just looks at me.

"Someone in this building—who I hope is still in this building—could endanger your country's security."

She'd never admit it, but her eyes have watered up a little. Looking in them, I know with certainty that she believes what she's saying. But I still don't close the blade. Just because she believes it doesn't mean I have to.

"Does this have something to do with the packages you claim to know nothing about?"

"Whether the rest of us like it or not, your country's vulnerability means ours as well, your enemies and allies alike. You're worried about five hundred people? I'm worried about seven billion. Please, Peter, don't do it. *Please*."

At first, I can't even process what she's saying to me, except the part about how the security of the planet rests with someone in this building. But then I hear the desperation in her voice. Just a second ago, she was pleading with Koval the same way. Was she being truthful with him then or me now? Or has she been lying to us both? But the way she's looking at me, I believe her. Just hope I don't regret it.

I loosen my grip around Koval's neck, but stay in position in case I need to put him under again. Or slit his throat.

Katie stands over Koval and pats him down. "Told you. No weapons."

"He'll come to in a couple of minutes. Ask him what you need to, but you're going to have to do it with me right here."

"Those girls—"

"Are at the end of the hall. They won't hear you."

Katie shakes her head. "Peter, it's classified, and I—"

"Nope. There is no way in hell I'm leaving you and this guy alone." I look dead into her eyes so she knows there will be no negotiating on this point.

Katie throws her hands in the air like she's just about done. "Because you still don't trust me?"

"Why should I? You still haven't told me anything—not enough, anyway," I say, feeling that jumble of roller-coaster nerves coming back. Katie can throw me off my game like no one else. "It's because I don't trust either of you, but also because if we really are on the same side, even without a weapon, this guy might kill you."

No sooner do I say it than Koval comes to life—about a minute earlier than I expected—and grabs the knife from my hand. My position for the sleeper hold means I'm now pinned beneath two hundred and fifty pounds of muscle. With a knife.

"Run, Katie!"

If I'm going out, at least I can provide a distraction until Katie can get Rachel and her crew safely back to a locked classroom.

But Rachel has other plans. Like Bunker, she has apparently watched too many movies, because from down the hall I hear her yell, "He can't take us all. Let's save Prettyboy!"

Koval rolls off of me and gets into a fighting stance, keeping one foot on my chest. But the sight of fifteen girls charging down the hall must make him realize he's outnumbered seventeen to one—with a switchblade as his only defense—because he looks down at me and back up at Katie before he runs for the nearest stairwell.

"Should we go after him?" Rachel asks.

"I am so grateful you saved me, but now y'all need to go back to your classroom, bolt the doors, and don't come out again until the police arrive."

But Katie has other ideas. "No, we *should* go after him. This may be my only chance—"

"He's probably gone for backup, and he won't have just my knife when he returns," I say.

"So you're in this, too?" Rachel asks Katie. "I mean, whatever Prettyboy is, you're one, too?"

"Yes. This is our job; they're coming for us. They won't hurt you if you stay out of their way. So you need to do as Peter asks and go back to your classroom."

Rachel nods, and it seems her friends finally get that this is serious business. A few of them wish us good luck before they all turn and run.

CHAPTER 22

As soon as the girls are gone, Katie heads for the stairwell, but I step in front of her.

"You don't know if he's lying in wait behind that door. For all we know, he could have a weapon stashed in there."

"But I need to confirm . . . something."

"Yeah, I know. Something about the package," I say, stepping so close we're almost touching. All I can think of is how I felt about Katie before I learned who she really is. "But you can't do that if you're dead."

When I take Katie's hand, I'm surprised she doesn't fight me. Maybe she's remembering me from before, too. I lead her around the corner into the next corridor, to the same stairwell Bunker and I took up to the roof.

"Let go of my hand," she says, sounding more like the Katie I know now. "Where are you taking me?"

"Uh, you're welcome? And by the way, we're even."

"Yes, well, thank you," she says before sitting on the bottom step to look through her bag, which she stopped to grab as we ran past the alcove.

"Truth time, Katie. If you aren't here for me, why are

you here? Why do you believe the whole planet is in jeopardy? And what's up with the 'package'? Don't play like you don't know."

"Truth time, Peter," she says without answering even one of my questions. "You say they're here to kill you. Okay, but why are *you* here?"

It's the same thing I was wondering about her, so I shouldn't be surprised she asks this, but I am. Since I don't want to reveal the hacker just yet, I don't have a ready answer.

"Just as I suspected. Assuming you really do work for the Americans, I'm here for the same reason. And rather than sit here in this stairwell playing *Trust Me, Trust Me Not,* we should be getting on with it. You brought me here because you know where the package is, right?"

I almost join her on the steps, but lean against the wall instead. Katie might still be lying. Not about being an operative—I've seen her in action, so she's clearly that— but she may not be one of the good guys. She has already fooled me once. Who's to say this isn't another cover, another lie? That's what my brain tells me.

It's mostly my heart that's having the crisis of confidence.

"If I agree to team up," Katie continues, apparently believing she's now running the show, "you'll need to step back once we get through this mess. We had him first, even if you did try playing nicey-nicey with him."

"*He's* a she," I correct her, letting her know psych games also won't work on me. Either that or I just gave away information she didn't have. "And what do you mean, you had her first?"

"Nothing. I didn't mean anything by it," she says, not that I believe her.

"Well, that's where we're going, to check on your—*our*—package. It's on the roof," I say, expecting this to clarify everything.

Katie looks confused.

"How did it get up there?"

"After chasing it all over the school, I finally caught the package and left it on the roof under Bunker's guard."

Katie eyes me suspiciously. "But I secured it myself. Why would it run all over the school? And why do you keep calling it *the package*? We've agreed we're after the same thing. Do you not trust me enough to tell me who exactly you're after?"

"I notice you haven't named it, either."

Katie stares at me for a second, no doubt trying to figure out her next move.

"All righty then. If the package is on the roof, let's go up to the roof. Lead the way, CIA."

"No, after you. Ladies first."

Now it's my turn to get a serious eye-roll from Katie, but she goes up ahead of me where I can keep an eye on her. Even when a spy looks like Katie, it's tough for an operative to trust another one.

Especially when a spy looks like Katie.

We haven't finished the first flight of stairs when my walkie-talkie phone buzzes.

"What's that? You've had a working phone all this time?" Katie says, her expression a mix of frustration and hope, at least until she sees the phone I pull from my bag.

"Truly, what *is* that? It must weigh five pounds. Wait . . .

don't tell me your people have stolen the time-portal scientist away from us, too?"

"The *who*? You guys have a time—"

"Oh, never mind," she says, looking like she's just been busted. I can't tell if she's messing with me or being serious. She casually waves in the direction of the phone. "So what's that about?"

"It isn't a real working cell phone. It's a two-way radio."

Then we hear a series of beeps: three quick beeps, a pause, two more beeps, a pause, and then one final beep.

"What is that—Morse code?"

"No, that's Bunker. It's a bad sign that he sent me an alert rather than calling me. He's saying, *I need cover.* Well, that's probably not exactly what he's saying, it's a thing we worked out for—it doesn't matter. I think it means Bunker's in trouble."

Katie follows me as I take the stairs two at a time. When we reach the roof, there is no sign of him. The only place to hide up here is behind the HVAC units, and neither Bunker nor the hacker is there.

"Oh no," I say again, and then two more times because it's all I can think to say. The wave of panic that just hit me has taken away my ability to think.

"So where are they?" Katie asks.

"I don't know. I left them right here. Bunker was here, and she was sitting right there next to that HVAC thing."

"Who is this *she* you keeping talking about?"

"The hacker, obviously."

"You thought the package was this hacker? Oh no. I have to find Koval," Katie says, sounding as afraid as I was when I found Bunker missing. She runs for the door we came through and returns a second later. "Peter, it's locked."

"Aw, damn! I was so worried about Bunker, I forgot to prop it open behind us."

"We should have gone after Koval when he ran into the stairwell. There's no telling where he is. He could be off campus by now."

"And risk taking a bullet the minute we opened that door? Besides, if he somehow left the campus in that short amount of time, that's a good thing. One less man to fight. And—dude was like two men."

She must not see the good fortune in Koval's possible departure because she's just sounding more panicked. "This girl you're looking for, she might know some-thing. Was she tied up? Sedated? What state did you leave her in?"

Katie's questions are starting to get on my nerves, but I'd be asking the same questions if the tables were turned.

"I didn't leave her in any state, none of those things. But I left Bunker to guard her."

"Oh, is he CIA, too?"

"No, but the girl's just a hacker, and I thought . . ."

"I assume 'hacker' is what you would put on your re-sume too, if you were sent to Carlisle to bring her in. From what I've seen of you so far, you're pretty handy away from the keyboard. You didn't think she might be as well?"

Okay. That's one question too many. Katie may be the first girl I could fall for, and her questions may be legit, but right now they aren't making me any less afraid for Bunker, and I can't help taking out my fear for my friend on her.

"Of course I'd have rather secured the hacker better and not have left her with a guy whose understanding of covert ops comes from watching James Bond movies. But I had to come rescue you," I say, not caring one iota whether I sound like a Neanderthal, or like I'm trying to pull the plug on her girl power, or whatever. "That's right. I said it. *Rescue.* It may not have happened that way and you may have ended up rescu—*helping* me, but when I left my best friend up here alone with a cyberterrorist, that's what I thought I was doing. I was leaving him to save Katie Carmichael, regular girl. I chose you over Bunker, and now who knows what the hell has happened to him."

At the end of my rant, Katie just stares at me for a second, probably thinking I've lost it, but then she takes my hand. She holds it for only a second, but the gesture calms us both down.

"Let's think this through," she says, sounding a lot more composed. "If this hacker has been controlling the school's security system, and she was able to overtake Bunker, she'd have locked the door to the roof. It's an escape route for you. She probably knows any operative worth his salt carries emergency rappelling equipment. So she wanted you to be up here for some reason."

"Or maybe she knows I'm the kind of spy who *doesn't* have any emergency rappelling equipment. But thanks for that."

"Nothing has happened to him, Peter. And we aren't going to let it."

They're nice words, and I really do appreciate the pep talk, but except for the zeroes and ones of cyberspace, I don't believe in anything I can't see.

And right now, what I see is Bunker's *Phantom Menace* backpack near the edge of the building, on the side facing the school's driveway. It looks innocent and lost up here on the empty roof, the way a little kid looks wandering around a department store alone, and causes the same reaction in me—I can feel Bunker's fear, his panic.

"That's his?" Katie asks, but she already knows the answer. She's just trying to distract me from noticing that she's trying to look over the edge of the roof.

"Go ahead. Check it out."

"The hacker may have wanted to make her getaway before any police arrived, and taken Bunker with her as a hostage," Katie offers. "They could have rappelled over."

"Just look, will you?"

It's the longest five seconds of my life.

"There's nothing, no one down there. She has to be somewhere in the building. We can—"

I don't wait to hear the rest of Katie's plan. I start walking the perimeter. Bunker's pack being here doesn't mean this is where he may have . . . left the roof. The U-shape of the building makes for a lot of roof edge.

"No, Peter," Katie calls after me. "I'll do it. You shouldn't be the one to—"

"I definitely should be the one. It's the very least I can do, since I'm the one who left him up here with someone I knew was dangerous," I say, because it's true. But I appreciate what Katie is trying to do, so I add, "You go left, I'll go right."

Katie tries to offer a smile, some comfort, but I can tell she's worried about finding the same thing I am. My stomach lurches, but I force myself to follow my own instructions and head right, covering the north-facing side of the building. With each yard of the roof's edge that I cover without finding any sign of Bunker, I am encouraged to cover the next yard.

I'm so busy looking down, I almost miss movement among the stand of Russian olive trees about three hundred yards south of Carlisle, near an old abandoned shed. It's such a small movement, and so brief, that I'm wondering if my eyes are playing tricks on me. I stand there watching, and I see it again—flecks of black moving among the light green leaves.

Then the flecks grow bigger as they emerge from the trees, and I know exactly what it is, even if I don't know whether it's good or bad.

It's a full-scale tactical incursion.

CHAPTER 23

From this distance, nothing gives away whether these people are friendly or hostile. They're dressed pretty much the same way I am, the same way black ops everywhere dress, which could make them military, mercenary, FBI, or even the SWAT team from the Boulder police department.

When Katie reaches me, she's smiling, which means she found no sign of Bunker being pushed off Carlisle's roof. My relief is deep, but only lasts a second because we now have a new problem. I motion to her to get down. She lies on her stomach, next to me.

"Katie, were you able to get the SOS out to your team before all comms went down?" I ask her.

"If I had, they'd be here by now."

I point in the direction of the Russian olive trees. "Well, someone's coming."

"I'm not sure if we should be relieved or worried," Katie says, pulling mini-binoculars from her purse. She clearly has a better go-bag than I do, and it appears to be bottomless.

"When in doubt, I always go with worry."

"They aren't part of an overt operation like local police or FBI," she says as she peers through the binoculars. "If they were, their affiliation would be stamped all over their clothes. Requirement for good community relations."

"You know who doesn't care a good goddamn about community relations? Terrorists. Mercenaries. We're not waiting until they get here to find out. You have rappelling equipment in your bag, right?"

"They could be special forces. They tend not to broadcast who they are." Katie is more hopeful than I am.

"Let me see," I say, motioning for her binoculars. By now the team is close enough that I clearly recognize the guy who appears to be the leader. White-blond hair, shockingly white skin, eyes so flinty gray it's almost like he has no irises—the kind of looks that make me wonder how he succeeds in a business that requires blending in. "There's one more organization that prefers anonymity. Mine."

"They're CIA? Are you sure? Neither of us were able to call for help. "

"I'm sure the lead guy is. His name's Berg. He was at Langley while I was in training, but was forward deployed a few months ago. Unless he's gone to the other side, that's a Company team."

"The fact that he's here makes me think his defection is a possibility. How would the CIA even know there's a problem?" Katie asks.

"I lied to my boss about why I wanted to attend Carlisle, but maybe she read right through my lie and figured I was here to track the hacker, and thought I needed help."

"But why today? It's too much of a coincidence."

"Maybe my team picked up some noise today about Marchuk's arrival?" I offer. My turn to be hopeful. Berg's an asshole, but he isn't a traitor.

I don't think.

Katie rolls away from the edge of the roof, out of sight of the approaching team, before she stands up and starts peeling off her clothes. It takes me a second to realize I probably shouldn't be staring like I've just seen the promised land, and turn back to look at the approaching agents. But I can't help but comment because, you know, *Katie*. Half naked.

"Hey girl, as much as I'd like to, this probably isn't a good time."

I can only imagine the eye-roll Katie's giving me when she says, "I'm glad you can find levity in our imminent capture. If they *are* your people, I don't want my cover blown. You can look now."

When I turn around, to my great disappointment, she is not half naked but back in her school-issued uniform, minus the blazer. It's a little wrinkled because it was no doubt crammed into that magical bag of hers, but she's back to looking like Katie Carmichael, Carlisle's most popular student.

"I'll keep your cover. Berg is the last person I'd do any favors for," I say, though I hope he'll do one for me. If it really is him, I could use a few of his people to help me find Bunker.

"You could be wrong and the leader just *looks* like the guy from your office. You were right to be worried. I don't think we should assume this is a rescue team."

It's too late for us to assume anything. Three soldiers,

CIA operatives, or Marchuk employees—I'm not sure which—have just come over the edge of the building, fully armed. No doubt there will be more right behind them. While we were busy looking north, another team roped up to the roof from the south. We might be screwed.

I stand to face Katie, with my arms up. Without turning around, she realizes what is happening and assumes the surrender position, too. We look at each other, silent for a moment, until Katie says, "Petah, I . . . I wouldn't have minded being your girlfriend."

"I should have asked you for a second date," I say, because I may never have the chance again.

But then I hear "Peter Smith!" being called from behind me without a trace of Ukrainian or English accent, just a good ol' plain-Jane Midwestern voice that I remember well.

"Ray Berg," I say, turning but keeping my arms up. I nod left, toward Katie. "It's okay. She knows who you are because I told her who I am."

Berg looks angry and dumbfounded at the same time.

"The whole damn world knows who you are. That's the problem," he says, his contempt for me obvious in every word. "And put your arms down. I'm here to save your ass, not kill you, though you tempt me."

"What do you mean, the whole world knows who I am?"

His response is so Berg, blowing the #Prettyboy thing way out of proportion. That's probably what he'll put in his report, too, exaggerating the situation just to keep me out of the service.

"Well, they don't know who you work for," Berg says. "Or who you *used* to work for, if I get my way. But they know what you look like. Did you cut class that day at

Langley? It's difficult to be a covert operative when your face is all over the internet."

"Hold up. You can't get me fired over that." It doesn't matter that I'm already close to being fired given my probationary status, but I'm not backing down from Berg on this because he's wrong. "For one, it isn't my fault. For two, I'm trending only in Denver. As long as I don't take any future assignments out here, I should be—"

"Only in Denver? Prettyboy, you're trending in the whole goddamn country."

"Seriously?" I think back to chem class, when Duncan first told me about my growing popularity. That was probably the moment my career ended, long before Berg threatened to end it. "I could have taken down that photo, scraped Twitter clean of any mention of Prettyboy before it blew up. But I chose between protecting my cover and, oh, five hundred people. Or does that not count for something with you, Berg?"

"This ain't high school, kid. You don't get a trophy for doing your job, especially when you created the problem. When thirty thousand people know your face, it's a good bet your Company work is done. Rogers should have left you in a cubicle, where all hackers should be. Except maybe for the one who led us here. You owe her a slice of pizza, or Katy Perry tickets, or whatever kids consider returning a favor these days."

There is so much wrong in what he just said, but I can only refute one error at a time, so I start with the most important one. "You think the hacker is the good guy in all this? She's the reason my best friend is missing."

"No, she's the reason we even know about all this. She

got word to us a few hours ago about an incursion happening here today."

"You've known about this for a few hours? Why didn't you move in earlier?" I ask.

"She provided irrefutable proof the lockdown had already happened. Said she could hack us inside if we give her some time. Took us an hour to mobilize, but we've been waiting to move in. She called me a few minutes ago to let me know this was the time to strike."

I bet she did. The moment Katie and I stepped out onto the roof.

"The incursion is most definitely not a hoax. The hacker, on the other hand—"

"If you're aware of the incursion, why are you out here on the roof instead of inside doing something about it?"

"I locked myself out," I say, barely audible.

"Say what? I didn't hear you."

"I locked myself out." This time, I almost shout it.

The hacker has been playing me all this time, from long before she called Berg this morning right up until I got that alert from Bunker. She wanted me up here on this roof, messed up in the head about Bunk and locked out by my own hand, when Berg arrived. Because she wanted revenge on me, too—not to kill me like Marchuk wanted, but to wreck my life the same way I wrecked hers.

"Because she wanted me to look like an idiot," I say aloud without meaning to.

"Well, if that's true, she succeeded. Take a look," Berg says, pointing toward the door, which an operative is holding open.

He slaps me on the back like we're old friends, laughing at me like this is all so hilarious. Berg has no idea, but if he keeps talking, it's about to be on. Problem is, he's armed and has a platoon of officers at his command. I have a Swiss Army knife and a sock of ball bearings in my backpack, which means unless I want to get dead, I have to use my words.

"Because she just unlocked it."

"Sure she did."

"The breach happened in my sixth-period class, but I've neutralized three of the six known hostiles."

"Actually, you've taken out four of them. Don't forget the one in the art supply closet," Katie adds, giving me credit for her takedown of the groundskeeper. I guess her cover isn't blown yet, and she'd like to keep it that way.

Berg looks at Katie as though it's the first time he's noticed her. He looks at me as though he doesn't believe anything we've told him so far.

"You took out four highly trained terrorists? All on your own?" Berg asks, but doesn't wait for me to answer. "That would explain that beating your face took, but not hers. Or did she help you?"

"Peter rescued me, sir," Katie says.

Berg is silent as he circles Katie and me, his arms crossed. I hope it's because he's actually listening to what I've been trying to tell him.

"Well, I know the hacker couldn't have helped you, since she isn't even in the country. At least you're well-trained, then. So Rogers did get *something* right with her pet project."

I want to call him out on that dig at Rogers and me, but I'm more concerned about the other thing.

"What do you mean, the hacker isn't even in the country?"

"Look, Smith, we have five hundred civilians in this building and by your count, we still have two hostiles unaccounted for. I should be the one asking you questions. Give me a quick assessment so we can get to work minimizing civilian casualties."

"There *are* no civilian casualties, thanks to Peter," Katie says, forgetting she's supposed to be playing a confused, terrified, and *quiet* Carlisle student. Her voice is full of attitude. English attitude still sounds too polite to be intimidating, but I appreciate her having my back.

Berg is probably about to ask who the hell she is, but he's interrupted by a phone call. His expression tells me he's not happy about it. He steps away, trying to keep me from hearing his end of the conversation, but returns a minute later, smiling.

"It's your boss," Berg says, putting Rogers on speaker-phone.

Finally, someone who isn't out to get me and might actually want to hear what I have to say.

"Peter, Officer Berg has already apprised me of the situation. It sounds like you've done an excellent job of containing the crisis, but it's time to step back and let Berg and his team take over."

"Ma'am, I don't know what Berg told you, but he seems to think the hacker is helping us, when she's the one who set this whole thing up," I say, trying to keep my voice even, because if I can't convince Rogers to believe me over Berg, I'm going to lose this fight. "She jammed our communications so we couldn't get help. She took over the school's network and security system to turn Carlisle into a prison for five hundred hostages."

"But Berg told me the hacker is the one who saved the day," Rogers says.

"No, *I* saved the day, with help from some friends, one of whom is probably in trouble right now. Two of the hostiles are contained in my chem lab, another is in the art supply closet. And the main prize is knocked out in the office—Pavlo Marchuk. And by the way, boss, a memo that he was out of hiding would have been nice."

Berg gives me a weird look, and there is silence on the other end of the line. I can tell they're both impressed. I know Rogers is trying to decide if she's making the right call by taking me out of the action. I keep going, trying to sell her on the idea that this is my project to finish, and even if Berg takes the lead I should still be part of his team.

"I did all of that without a single civilian casualty. Doesn't that prove I'm capable of helping Berg see this thing through?"

"Officer Berg, please take me off speakerphone and let me talk to Peter alone."

Berg does as he's instructed, with a smile, because he thinks he just won. I snatch the phone from him, barely able to wait until Rogers gives me an order that will wipe that smile right off his face.

"All of that is very impressive, Peter," Rogers says as I start to walk away from Berg. He grabs my arm to stop me, and comes this close to getting knocked the hell out, but I let it go.

"So I should be part of the team, right? He thinks the hacker—"

"Enough with the hacker, Jake." I know she's getting ticked off now, since she's using my real name. "Don't you see that your obsession with the hacker is what put those five hundred people in danger in the first place? Your mission to chase down the hacker led you to Carlisle. Marchuk's mission to take revenge on you led *him* to Carlisle. We called, tried to warn you there was intel he may have surfaced, but you chose to ignore us."

"No way. I wouldn't have ignored . . . the hacker must have intercepted the message—"

"We all know why the breach happened in *your* classroom."

"Boss, just give me one more chance to prove—"

"Jake, stop. It's over. I truly appreciate you keeping the school safe until help arrived, but it's time to step back. That's an order."

She disconnects without even saying goodbye. I hand the phone back to Berg. He's right. He has won.

"Do what your boss says and don't give me any trouble. Time to let the grown-ups take over."

CHAPTER 24

I'm about to go off on Berg for the second time, but Katie jumps in front of me. I guess she knows me well enough to see what was about to go down, even if Berg didn't. He's too smug, too certain I'm a boy playing a man's game, to think I could ever be a threat to him. Katie gives me a look that says, *You won't win this way,* and I stand down. I let her lead me away from Berg and over to the spot where I'd left my best friend to guard a terrorist.

"We need to convince Berg about Bunker," I say.

"He thinks the hacker is some knight in shining armor. There's no way he's going to believe us about Bunker. We'll have to find them ourselves."

Now that the adrenaline rush of wanting to do serious damage to Berg's face has subsided, I'm beginning to wonder if his assessment of me isn't too far off the mark.

"How am I going to do that, Katie? I should never have left him alone with her in the first place. I should never have—"

"Chosen me over him?" Katie says, finishing my thought. "You didn't choose. You did what we do. Analyzed the situation, ran a quick risk assessment, figured out which situation most required your action. At the time, you didn't know I was an operative who could take care of herself. You left Bunker to guard a seven-stone girl who you'd already contained. You made the same call I or any operative would have."

I feel the walkie-phone buzzing again.

"It's Bunker!" I say, pulling it from my backpack.

Again we hear a series of beeps.

"Okay, *that* was Morse code, and it was the best thing I've heard all day," I say. "You heard what I heard, didn't you?"

"*Sorry, Peter, but she got away,*" Katie says. "Though I'm not sure why this news has you smiling like that."

"Because Bunker is okay!" Capturing the hacker is all I've wanted for months, right up until the moment I thought my best friend was dead.

"Why didn't he just call you?" Katie asks.

"When he first gave me the radio, he was worried Marchuk's people might use the same channel."

"I guess we have to hope they don't know Morse code. Come to think of it, why does Bunker?"

"If you knew his father, you'd understand."

She doesn't look nearly as relieved as I am about the message, but then she hardly knows Bunker. Also, I've never seen an operative with such singular focus as Katie.

"Now that Bunker's safe, I really need to get back inside to check on something."

"So . . . we're still working together, then?"

She hesitates before offering me her hand. Instead of shaking it, I grab Katie and hug her. Maybe it's knowing

Bunker's okay, but I'm caught up in my feelings. I mean really caught up, because I don't let go for a few seconds.

"Whoa, Smith. Berg will probably consider that conduct unbecoming to an operative," she says before I let her go.

I don't think she really minded the contact, but Katie reminds me I have other problems. I watch all the activity around me. Berg giving orders to his team leaders as they review Carlisle's blueprints. Officers checking their gear and waiting for directives. Still more SWAT officers arriving over the roof's edge.

"Your package. Who is it really?"

Katie is about to say something, but stops. We're both quiet a moment and then she leads me to the edge of the roof. "Look. It's begun."

And it has. The first wave of kids is being led out of the building, which means the hacker has released Carlisle's security system, though Berg and my boss don't know—and will probably never believe—that she was the one who hijacked it in the first place. Still, seeing the first of my schoolmates getting out safely makes me think it'll all work out.

"I'll show you who the package is. At least, I hope he's still there and that Koval hasn't escaped with him. But that's *my* mission. I won't bring the CIA in on it unless I absolutely have to. I'll tell only you because I could use your help."

"Whatever you need, Katie."

"First, we have to get back inside the school. And if the person I'm protecting isn't where I left him, we'll need to find the hacker and question her before Berg gets a chance. She may know something."

She nods in the direction behind me.

"Look. That cop posted at the door just walked away to talk to Berg. Their backs are to us."

We quickly head for the unguarded door, and with Katie beside me I feel like we can do this. So of course, in keeping with the rest of this suck-fest of a day, someone tries to stop us. We're just a yard away from freedom when Berg turns around and spots us.

"Where do you two think you're going?" he asks, blocking our way.

Katie offers an explanation before I can. "We're going—"

"That was a rhetorical question. I know exactly where you're both going. You'll be evacuating with the rest of the school," Berg says, pointing at Katie. "The media has just caught on to this and will be here any minute. The parents will be next to arrive, and you'll be going home with yours. So say goodbye to your boyfriend."

"Say goodbye?" Katie asks.

"He's leaving town with us," Berg announces, which is news to me.

"Wait a minute, Berg. You can't just run me out of town."

"Your boss says I can. She wants you on the next plane to Virginia the minute I finish debriefing you."

I have reached my breaking point with Berg. "I don't give a damn what she said. I ain't getting on nobody's plane until—"

Katie grabs my arm. "What do you mean, officer? Shouldn't we both be evacuating with the school? Where are you taking him?"

Berg looks at Katie like he might actually have a heart, but must change his mind because he snaps his fingers in the direction of an officer and orders him to take Katie away.

"But I don't understand," Katie wails, turning on the waterworks instantly. "Where are you taking him?"

It's a wonder she didn't go out for drama club. Only a girl as smart as Katie can be this brilliant at playing dumb. But I'm the only who knows, just like I'm the only one who can decipher the look she gives me before she disappears behind the door to the stairwell with the officer: *Don't worry. I'm not going anywhere.*

"She's a bit dramatic. You sure know how to pick 'em. At least she's hot. I guess I shouldn't say that unless she's eighteen." Berg looks at me like he's thinking about what he just said—I hope he's regretting it. But no. "Wait, *is* she eighteen?"

Dude is about to get the beatdown I never got the chance to give Marchuk or Koval, but I try to stay on point, no matter how difficult Berg tries to make that.

"I can't go anywhere until I find out . . . find my friend." I almost said *find out who the package is,* but catch myself.

"That's your problem right there. Operatives don't have friends. And the local PD will find him. Or is that one a girl, too?" Berg winks at me, but doesn't wait for an answer. He gestures toward the edge of the roof. "Go take a look. Lots more of them should be rolling up right now."

"You can't trust the local cops. Or at least not one of them—Officer Andrews. She's in on it with Marchuk."

Berg stares at me for a second before he laughs.

"I'll give you one thing, kid—you're more paranoid than any spy I know, which is saying something. I never like the locals either, but calling them dirty? That's just clichéd."

"This isn't paranoia. This is truth. Soon as you talk to Headmistress Dodson, she'll confirm—"

"Operation Early Bird," he says, shaking his head and waving over someone behind me. "How the hell did Rogers ever think that was a good idea?"

I start to protest, but he whistles—drowning out my words—and signals another uniform to come over.

Berg instructs, "Put him in your squad car and make sure he can't get out."

The local starts handcuffing me but Berg stops her.

"No cuffs. As much as I hate the idea of it, he's one of us. He won't fight you," Berg says, giving me a look that says I better not even think about it. "Just make sure he stays put."

The officer ushers me downstairs and outside, where I've wanted to be ever since I realized the school had been turned into a prison. You'd think I'd feel relieved to finally be out of the building, even if I'm locked in a squad car. I feel anything but.

I check my phone and find I have a weak signal. The car must be parked far enough from the hacker's signal blocker, or else Berg's team found and disengaged it.

Rogers answers on the first ring.

"Jake, we cannot have this discussion," she says before I can even say hello.

"It isn't about Berg, or the hacker, or even about Marchuk. It's about his father's second-in-command."

"His son was second-in-command. We knew that even in Ukraine."

"But this other guy was supposed to have the job. He's the really dangerous one, and he's after something way bigger than me. I was just about to learn what—or who—it is when Berg—"

"I'm not there, Jake, and this is not my operation. I have to defer to the team on the ground, and you do, too."

"If Berg would just let me talk to—"

"Be careful, Jake. Berg is gunning for me. He's anti–Operation Early Bird in general, and anti-*you* in particular."

"Yeah, he made that pretty clear."

"Then you know you have to stand down."

"But—"

The line goes dead.

I stare out at the stand of Russian olive trees Berg and his team hid behind, feeling as abandoned as that old shed I'd seen from the roof.

Then my phone vibrates in my pocket.

The text is just a single sentence.

If you want him to live, come to the sub-basement.

CHAPTER 25

So the hacker still has Bunker after all. It has to be her. Something felt off about that Morse-code message, but I was so happy to hear he was okay that I immediately dismissed it. And now I know what it was. The message said, *Sorry, Peter.* Even though he was worried about the bad guys using the same channel, in a stressful situation like that, I think Bunker would have called me Jake. Back in the library, he said from now on, I was going to be Jake Morrow to him.

Berg stopped Katie before she could tell me why she's really at Carlisle, then took my mission away. Rogers was so worried about her stupid career she wouldn't even listen to what may be the biggest piece of intel she'll ever receive. Well, they can both go straight to hell and take my job with them, because I don't need to be a CIA employee to save my best friend.

That's exactly what I'm going to do, if I can just figure out how to get out of this police car.

All I have in my pockets are a cigarette lighter and the Sharpie. Koval took the switchblade, and my Swiss Army knife was in my backpack. Even if Berg hadn't confiscated my bag and I had all my tools with me, I don't think the locks on police cars are pickable. At least my hands are free, not that they're doing me any good. Next I try kicking the door open, but I can't get enough leverage to build sufficient force. I consider kicking out the glass, but Berg would probably lose any patience he had left with me and have me taken into lockup, and then I would have zero chance of saving Bunker.

Shouldn't this have been on the syllabus at Langley? Freeing Yourself From a Locked Squad Car 101 would have been just as useful as those classes on dirty bombs and money laundering. I have been frustrated too many times to count today, but not being able to escape this stupid car seems to be the straw that will break my back.

All I can do is sit on the wrong side of the squad-car window, freezing in the air conditioning thanks to the officer who left the engine running, watching my freed classmates stream past me. I hope they don't think I'm some kind of criminal, that I was part of this whole thing. I raise my hands to the window, hoping they notice I'm not wearing cuffs. A few people smile at me even if they can't do anything to help, but not everyone's a fan. Through one of the windows the officer cracked open to keep me from dying of carbon monoxide poisoning, I hear one guy yell out, "Prettyboy sucks."

Oh, it's *that* guy. The one from the library.

Just when I'm about ready to give up, I notice Katie is part of the current line of people streaming past me. Rachel is walking ahead of her, and I see them whispering.

Rachel yells, "No, *you* suck," at the library dickhead before she hauls off and hits him. When he acts like he might hit her back, I see Duncan come to her defense. And as is the way of high schools everywhere, suddenly everyone is circling the two guys, chanting, "Fight! Fight!" which sends my guard over to break it up.

No one even notices Katie sneak over toward my make-shift prison, slip around to the other side of the car, out of sight, and open the door.

"Now that the civilians have been evacuated, they're going to a hard lockdown so they can look for the remaining hostiles," Katie says to me as though we've never been separated. I appreciate her not mentioning I'd basically been foiled by a child-safety lock.

"The hacker texted me. She's inside. She has Bunker," I tell her.

Katie stays in her crouched position outside the car and looks at me for a second. I expect her to say she was right to question Bunker sending a message in Morse code, but all she says is, "Do you think Koval is with them? I'm still worried he'll get to my asset before I do."

I appreciate that, too.

"There's a good chance he is. So let's stop him before he does," I say, starting to feel the confidence I had on the roof now that Katie and I are together again.

"It'll be hard getting in. There will be a guard at every entrance."

"What are your feelings on air ducts?" I ask, crouching down beside her as we use the squad car for cover. "Carlisle's are pretty nice. Heavier gauge steel, extra wide so they're easier to crawl through."

"I'm sold. The place is crawling with police. But trying

to access one of the air shafts from out here won't be cake, either."

"The hacker has Bunk in the basement, so we just need to find a vent leading there and drop down."

Katie looks at me like she is no longer sold on the idea, but says, "At least it's only one floor."

"Too bad Rachel's not around. We'll still need a distraction and she's pretty good at creating them. I'm sure Berg's team is keeping a close eye on all exit points."

Katie pulls the ponytail thing from her hair and shakes it out, like a girl in a shampoo commercial. "With some slight modifications to my uniform—hike up the skirt a few inches, undo a button or two—I could probably provide the distraction."

I cosign a hundred percent, but I don't tell her that, or mention she could keep her uniform at dress code requirements and still cause a distraction if she does that hair thing again in front of the right cop.

"We still need tools to open the vent cover," I tell her. "This line of squad cars will provide enough cover to reach the groundskeeper's shed. We can grab some tools and go from there."

We're able to reach the shed undetected. The whole place smells of creosote.

"Hey, you know you still owe me some intel, right?" I remind her.

"I don't *owe* you anything. I was going to *offer* you intel," she says, sounding like she's had a change of heart.

"And now?"

"We need to find our way into the building to see

whether it even matters anymore. Maybe the pretend groundskeeper hid some weapons in here?" Katie says, looking around the shelves.

I'm about to call her out on reneging on an agreement, but something else distracts me.

"Or maybe he was planning to make some. There's a lot of fertilizer stacked in this corner."

"The guy works for an arms terrorist. I'm pretty sure he didn't need to resort to homemade bombs."

"Yeah, you're probably right," I say, but I'm not convinced. I've seen a truck from one of those lawn fertilizer companies come out and spray the stuff in liquid form here. If these bags weren't stacked with plans to make Carlisle's grass as green as it is in the brochures, or to create bombs, then they were put here for some other purpose. "There's so much, though. It's like a wall of fertilizer. Maybe something's behind it?"

The top half of the last stack of bags has fallen over—or has been knocked over—allowing me just enough space to squeeze between the fertilizer wall and the real one.

"You can stop fussing with those bags," Katie says. "I found a screwdriver set. Perfect for opening vents. And for stopping bad guys from a distance if thrown with enough velocity and the right trajectory."

"I found something even better."

"Real weapons?"

"No, a trap door," I say.

After she presses through the narrow space to join me, Katie asks, "Why would the school put a trap door in the groundskeeper's shed?"

"I don't think they did. The door looks newer than the rest of the floor. This has to be the groundskeeper's doing."

Like a Girl Scout, Katie whips out a full-size Maglite and shines it down into the hole revealed by the opened trap door. It's probably three feet in diameter, just wide enough to let a man who bench-presses railroad ties fit through.

"It doesn't look like he got the chance to finish it." Katie gives me a look like she knows what I'm about to suggest, and is very afraid. "It's just a hole in the ground."

"Depends on where it leads. You were right when you said he smelled like the outdoors. He had a way to move in and out, even during the lockdown. He didn't need it to be pretty. He just needed to get from point A to point B undetected. Like we do."

Katie looks horrified, like I just asked her to jump into a pit of poisonous snakes.

"I really want to help you find this hacker and your best friend, but you're crazy if you think I'm going down there."

"And your asset. We're looking for him, too."

Katie considers this and looks like she might go along with the program, but then says, "It isn't even reinforced, and it's probably unstable. The earth could shift, and next thing you know, we're in our graves. Sorry, but no."

It's the first time I've seen Katie afraid of anything. She usually plays it so cool, but right now, she sounds the complete opposite, her voice climbing higher with every word.

"You're claustrophobic?"

"I am not."

"You have a fear of tunnels?"

"No, I have a fear of dying," Katie says, looking a little wild-eyed.

"That's a fear all field operatives learn to manage or we'd never go to work in the morning. How did you manage to get through the class on tunnel countermeasures?"

Katie looks at me like she's thinking of a lie to tell, but then decides on the truth. "The instructor was a young officer and I was—well—I flirted my way out of the class. Look, I'm not proud of it. And I'm also not going into that hole."

"It's okay. Don't worry—" I start, but stop myself because I know those are fighting words with Katie. "You stay here. I'll see where it leads. If I'm not back in five minutes, you'll know it led me inside Carlisle. If I'm not back in an hour, you'll know I'm worm food."

Katie punches me in the upper arm. Hard.

"Don't even joke like that. You'd *better* be back in five minutes, or I'll go to Berg. Take these," she says, removing a couple of the screwdrivers from the set she found in the shed. "I hope your throwing skills are good. You may need them."

We stare at each other for a moment, and I remember our one date, our first kiss, and I want to kiss her again because maybe I'm not wrong about the tunnel and the worm-food thing. But that's a distraction I don't need right now.

I step away because I can tell she's distracted too, and before she can mount a protest, I let myself fall down into the hole.

CHAPTER 26

Now I understand the groundskeeper's fascination with railroad ties. He wasn't using them just for weightlifting or landscaping. He was using them to brace the dirt walls. But even knowing the tunnel is somewhat reinforced, I have to agree with Katie—this is not my favorite place. I try to think of it as no different than scrambling through an air shaft, but now I've got Katie's words in my head about the whole thing collapsing and becoming my grave.

Especially when I hear a sudden rumbling noise overhead. For a second, I'm certain it's an earthquake and I'm about to die. Then I remember they generally don't have earthquakes in Colorado. I must be underneath a road, which doesn't make me feel better. Two-ton SUVs driving over a makeshift tunnel can't be good for it. To keep from losing my nerve, I remind myself that I'm doing this for Bunker, and it isn't that far of a distance between the tool shed and the main building—and that I refuse to lose face after talking smack to Katie about her tunnel phobia—and I just keep moving forward.

Forty-five seconds later, I'm relieved to still be among the living when I find the tunnel ends at another trap door only a foot above my head. I have to hope that wherever I am, one of Berg's rescue team isn't. Or that I can even open the trap door at all. It might be covered with bags of fertilizer.

I lift the door just far enough to see if the room is occupied. I'm hella relieved to find it isn't.

Once I open it completely and pull myself up into the room, I see that it's—no surprise here—the janitor's office. The door was hidden by a rug. The tunnel must have been some kind of escape route in case things went bad. From here, I just need to go a few steps to reach the stairwell to the sub-basement.

I have no idea where the hacker will be down there. The only weapons I have are my hands, feet, and the screwdrivers Katie gave me. Any of them are deadly in hand-to-hand combat, but I'm hoping I don't have to get that close. Even if the hacker's been trained by the Russians and is the most skilled level-five Spetsnaz fighter ever, I have nearly a hundred pounds and more than a foot on her, and I ain't too bad at the kickass myself. But if Koval is still on campus with her . . . I don't ever want to go hand-to-hand with that guy again. The tools could be used as throwing weapons, but you need the right amount of distance to throw with enough velocity to make them lethal.

At the door I hesitate, preparing myself just in case Koval is behind it, along with the hacker and Bunk.

"What are you waiting for, Peter? The door is unlocked," the hacker says from the other side of it.

I look up to find a security camera mounted on the wall behind me. Right. She's probably been watching me since

I hit the stairwell. I've lost the element of surprise, but I'm glad I didn't take out the screwdriver that's hidden inside my sleeve, in preparation for an attack. At least she doesn't know whether I'm armed.

When I open the door, the first thing I see is Medusa standing behind my best friend, one hand waving her smart-watch at me, the other pointing a rifle at his back. She has him gagged so he can't say anything, but I can tell from his eyes that he's terrified.

I have never hated anyone, even Duncan before he morphed into a human. But this girl? She ought to be glad I'm not armed or she would be so dead right now.

"Aren't these things the best?" she says. "I could monitor your approach even with my hands full. I'll admit I was a little worried there for a minute."

"Like you'd ever worry about Bunker."

"Bunker? Oh, you mean him," she says, jabbing the barrel of her rifle into his back, making his eyes widen beyond what you'd think humanly possible. "Of course not. I was worried about *me*. Or more specifically, I was worried about my plan. But you made it to the party. I didn't think you would after that Berg person had you locked up."

"So you're listening in on his every move, huh?"

"He thinks I'm in London. What a moron. If that is what passes for leadership in your organization, then this whole thing should be so easy."

"What whole thing?"

"Koval taking his rightful place. He's been second-in-command for years. But then you found the list and exposed our clients. You ruined my reputation, and because he brought me into Marchuk's organization, you ruined his, as well."

By the time she finishes the last sentence, her English accent is gone. Koval had said she could affect a number of accents, but it's clear this was the one she grew up speaking.

"So you're Ukrainian, too, not some English hack-for-hire working for Marchuk?"

She doesn't answer, but I want to keep her calm and talking while I work out a plan.

"You work for Koval now?"

"I was always on his side. Vadim Koval is my brother. And this has always been *my* plan. Sveta works for no one but herself."

"What exactly is this plan of yours?" I take a small step back, hoping she'll subconsciously respond to my movement by stepping forward. So far, all I can think to do is draw her near enough to me to disarm her, then take her out with hand-to-hand combat. But she doesn't move, just stays there with that rifle muzzle pressed against Bunker's back.

"You are so smart, haven't you figured it out? No, because I'm smarter. I suppose it doesn't matter if I tell you now. Who are you going to tell, Prettyboy? No one, because you'll soon be dead." She smirks at that last part, which actually makes me hopeful. Her overconfidence is a weakness to exploit. "We would get your people to capture, hopefully kill Marchuk, since we all know the capturing didn't go so well last time."

So they wanted the CIA to do their dirty work. I just hadn't realized how far back the plan went. Sveta has played me for a fool for even longer than I believed.

"So you're saying even back in the Ukraine, you were manipulating us into taking out Marchuk for you?"

"We wanted either the clients or the CIA to do it, as long as Vadim continued to look like the grieving, loyal sergeant. But both you and the clients failed. Well, you did get the old man."

"And here I thought Koval was just waiting for Marchuk Senior to retire so he could inherit the business. But y'all planned all along to take it from *both* Marchuks, except making their clients believe our people killed them."

"You let the stupid one get away," Sveta continues, "but I lured him out of hiding—"

"And I suppose it was with your help that I didn't know anything about that?" I ask, still stalling for time, still hoping I can draw her close enough to kill her with my bare hands, or at least away from Bunker so I can throw a screwdriver into her heart. Fortunately, people love talking about themselves, especially sociopathic people who think they're extra brilliant and underappreciated. I take a small step forward. Sveta is so into bragging about herself, she doesn't notice.

"Yes. I intercepted recent calls, voicemail, and texts from the CIA, just letting through what I wanted you to see," Sveta boasts, clearly proud of her phreaking skills. If Bunker's eyes weren't starting to water out of fear that she's about to kill him, I'd admit to her that I'm impressed. "Vadim has been working to get the operation up and running again while that coward Marchuk hid out, just waiting to surface and take over again. So I hurried things along."

"You know he isn't dead, right?" I ask, closing my fingers

around the handle of the Phillips-head inside my sleeve, waiting for the moment I can use it.

"For now. Your people have been embarrassed by Marchuk. I doubt they'll let that happen again. They'll either kill him by accident, or at the very least, make sure he never escapes again. Vadim and I will take over permanently, as it should have been before you destroyed everything. Or tried to. Today will make everything right again. You showing up was just a bonus."

"You lured me here!"

"I didn't know what you looked like. It was Marchuk who saw you in the student directory. He wanted to kill you. I wanted to ruin you. And Vadim wanted to use you as CIA bait. All you did was help. And you had no idea."

"So you took the photo of me hoping it would go viral and get me burned out of the CIA for good, right? Or do you just have a thing for me?"

Sveta smiles at that, which hopefully means I'm distracting her enough to charge her.

"You're half right."

"So what's the other half of the story? What did you plan to do with me if you *had* found me in the chem lab? What other reason is there to make my photo go viral?"

"The photo was meant to scare your people into coming here and finishing what they started in Ukraine. Having your cover blown and making sure they knew Marchuk was in town assured that. It would be bad publicity if your government knew the CIA was employing teenage operatives on US soil. Spies dislike all publicity, no? Taking you as a hostage was the ace card, as you *Amerikanski* say."

"You took over an entire *school*," I say. "The authorities

would have come running, with or without me as your hostage."

"We didn't want just any 'authorities.' We needed the same organization that took out the old man, so it would look like they were finishing the job. Many people want Junior gone. Clients might suspect Vadim was one of them—after all, the job would have been his if not for . . ." Sveta doesn't finish, because it would mean admitting a time when she wasn't smarter than me. That pause makes her look away for one second, allowing me to move another step closer. "Anyway, we needed our customers to believe the CIA finished him off. I mean, do you really think people would believe you took out Marchuk and his team single-handedly?"

When I don't say anything, proving her right, she laughs.

"That is why the plan worked so well. You were so convinced the attack was about you, Prettyboy, you never saw the real threat coming. Do you think I would do all this to chase you here, to this country, *just* to ruin you?" She points the rifle at me. "I could have done that without either of us leaving Ukraine."

She's got a point there.

"Marchuk does not give a damn about you. Well, yes, he wanted to kill you," she muses as she circles Bunker, never taking her eyes off me, "but avenging his father wasn't enough to come out of hiding and put himself on American soil for easy capture. I gave him better bait."

"Better bait? What are you talking about?"

It must be the bigger thing Katie still hasn't told me about. The package. Which means I have absolutely zero leverage here because I was never critical to this mission.

Marchuk might have wanted me brought in alive so he could kill me himself, but he's probably in Berg's custody by now. I am of no use to Sveta or Koval at this point.

Sveta laughs, and I swear it is the laugh of a cartoon evil queen, but she doesn't answer my question.

"Now that I've told you all my secrets, I have to kill you. And obviously, I'll have to kill your friend, since he just heard all of that."

"Wait a minute. Maybe we can work something out," I say, reciting the desperate plea of captives everywhere.

"I know. It's really too bad I have to kill you. You're both so cute, and this one with the crush on me and all. But it must be done."

Then the crazy chick starts singing a kid's chant to figure out which of us she will shoot first. I'm going to die at the hands of a psycho, and the last words I'll ever hear will be *duck, duck, goose.*

CHAPTER 27

In the child's game, she would be circling both Bunker and me, but Sveta isn't stupid. She remains behind Bunker and keeps her distance from me. I'd hit Bunker, not her, if I threw the Phillips-head. If I charged, she'd squeeze off several rounds into me before I even took a second step. And then she'd kill Bunker before my body hit the floor.

I look at Bunker and the only thing I see in his eyes is him pleading with me to get us out of this thing. My last thought is going to be how I broke the few promises I've ever made to him.

"I'm so sorry," I say to my first and last true friend. "I wish I hadn't gotten you mixed up in this."

Just as Sveta is at her third *duck*, Katie falls through the ceiling and onto the psycho's back.

Sveta is thrown off-balance, and before she can figure out what just happened, Katie has the girl on the ground, her arm around Sveta's neck in a death grip. It takes a second to hit me that I'm not going to die today, or at least not in this moment, before I realize Sveta just might.

"Whoa, Katie. We need her alive."

"I'm not telling you anything," Sveta says as best she can with Katie's forearm crushing her windpipe.

"Don't get it twisted. I'll make you talk," I tell her.

But my first priority is freeing Bunker, and when I do, before I can even remove his gag, he hugs me like I haven't been hugged since my parents died. Out of all the foster homes I ever lived in—even where the parents cared something about me—and in all the group homes, and even the makeshift families on the street who adopted me when I was homeless, no one hugged me like this. So I hug him back. But only for a second because Katie is watching, and this isn't something operatives do unless it's part of a con. And even if she wasn't looking, I'm more messed up than Bunker knows, and that much . . . trust . . . from a person is more than I can handle in a single dose.

Or maybe Bunker does know, because he gives me a quick back-pat and steps way back from me.

"We got her," he says after removing his gag.

"Hate to admit it, but I think *she* got her. I guess I'm back to owing you one, Katie."

"No. I mean we *have* her. See," Bunker says, pulling his walkie-phone out of his pocket, "I recorded the whole thing. Before I let her get the best of me, I switched on the recorder. She's going down."

"Are you serious? That is outstanding, Bunker. You make one helluva partner."

Bunker is cheesing so hard, you wouldn't think the guy had been holding back tears just a couple of minutes ago.

"I take it Koval isn't here, then?" Katie asks.

"No. I was going to ask her about—"

But before I can, Katie sticks her with a needle.

Sveta laughs feebly before she says, "Doesn't matter. You're too late."

"What do you mean?" I ask, but Sveta's out cold.

"Why'd you do that, Katie?"

"Koval isn't here; she wasn't going to reveal anything about him or my asset, so we have no use for her."

"Yeah, about that. You'd best start talking, MI6."

"Oh, wait, are you serious?" Bunker interrupts. "Katie's a British spy? That is so—"

Katie looks like she wants to lay me out. "I cannot believe you just blew my cover."

"I'm going to tell him a bunch of other stuff about you if you don't start speaking truth. Right now."

Katie grabs my arm and pulls me away from Bunker. "Not in front of him."

"That's cool. Go ahead, take a minute. I'll just hang out here in this chair I almost died in. I don't need to know your spy secrets. You'd probably have to kill me if you told me, right?" Bunker laughs at his own joke, probably trying to work himself down from the case of nerves that comes with almost being killed.

"Who are you here to protect?" I ask once we're out of earshot of Bunker, but Katie doesn't answer. "If you're really on the right side of this thing, you need to trust me. You have to tell me or I can't help you."

"Who said I needed your help? I think you're misremembering the events of the last hour. As I recall you were tied to a chair, about to be tortured."

"Nothing like almost dying together to build trust."

"*I* was never in danger of dying."

"Have you forgotten Koval?"

"I would have gotten out of that. You didn't give me the chance."

She takes a seat on a workbench and goes quiet again as she starts looking through her bag, pulling out stuff in search of something that must be buried at the bottom. When she pulls out the pencil case, I reflexively take a defensive stance.

"Oh my God, Peter. I'm not going to sedate you. I'm just taking inventory. And if you could just be quiet for a moment while I think this out, that would be dandy."

It isn't like we have all the time in the world; but the day has been a shocker for both of us, so I give her a few minutes to think. It gives me a chance to reassess, too, starting from the beginning.

The hostiles have only breached one classroom, as far as I know. Since it was my chem class, no one can blame me for thinking they were after me, even if the hacker, Marchuk, and Katie want to act like I think I'm all that.

So if they didn't drop through my chem lab ceiling for me, who were they after? Just about every student at Carlisle could be a target if the hostiles were looking to kidnap and ransom for money. Marchuk needs to fund his terrorist activities. Maybe he figured he could kill two birds with one stone—or one Peter Smith with one bullet, in this case—ransom a rich kid and kill me, too. If that's what he wanted, the gold-mine heiress who sits in the front row of my class would be the perfect target.

But Katie said the asset is a "him." And I'm pretty sure *she* isn't here to kidnap and ransom a rich kid if she's really who she says she is. While the whole monarchy thing must be crazy expensive for them to keep going, surely the British government isn't that desperate for money. And the asset is someone Katie alleges I made "nicey-nicey" with, which definitely rules out Duncan, despite the fact that he's mad rich. I mentally scan my chem class-room.

Of course—how did I miss it?

We all arrived at Carlisle this semester—Katie, me, and the hacker, though she played the role of a freshman, which removed her from my suspect list. That means the target is also a new arrival, an American who'd affected a mild English accent because he'd spent the last three years there. The kid whose father is working on encryption codes to secure our nuclear defense system. How could I not have seen it when he'd been sitting right next to me for the last eight weeks? To my credit, it *had* been one of my earlier theories.

"Marchuk wasn't here for me. Or . . . at least not only for me. He's here for Joel Easter. And so are you."

I know I'm right the second Katie closes her pencil box, throws it into her bag, and stands to leave. I block her way, which I know by now is probably a bad idea, but I take my chances.

"Are you going to let me by or will I have to hurt you?" Katie asks.

"Just wait a second, will you? Our missions are clearly linked. How is yours tied to Marchuk?"

"I'd never heard of Marchuk until today. My people picked up some chatter about a most-wanted arms dealer landing at Denver International yesterday."

"That must have been the chatter Sveta wanted both of our countries to hear—Berg's irrefutable proof."

"We didn't have any details—name, photo, anything—so standard protocol was for all operatives in the area to go on high alert."

"All operatives? How many MI6 are in Denver, anyway?"

"I suspect far fewer than the number of CIA that are currently in, oh, Manchester, let's say. Knowing all your friend's secrets strengthens the bond. Speaking of which, you still haven't told me everything about this hacker."

"She's helping Marchuk—well, Koval—go after Joel. I guess you know about the work Joel's dad is doing."

"Of course. He was doing it for us before your country lured him away. I can assure you that it will be bad for both our countries—pretty much the whole world—if Koval gets hold of that encryption technology."

"Whoever gets that information might be able to access our weapons systems—"

"And ours. Remember, we had him first," Katie says.

"This thing is bigger than us or our countries. I see why you were worried about all seven billion of us. Terrorists could gain access to the most powerful weapons arsenal in the world. Well, I mean, access to *two* of the most powerful arsenals in the world."

We both know that comparing our military capacity to theirs is like comparing a shoulder-launched surface-to-air missile to a Super Soaker, but I figure it doesn't hurt to throw Katie and the Brits a bone. I figure wrong.

"Do you know what I hate more than guys telling me not to worry?" Katie asks.

"Um, no?" Actually, I do, because I saw what happened to Marchuk.

"Guys condescending to me. Now get out of my way before I make you regret doing that."

I do, but with every intention of following her, because in all my worrying about the matchbook stuck in the front door, then Duncan sitting in my seat and harassing me about the Twitter thing, I didn't notice that Joel wasn't at my table today.

"You went AWOL during the fire drill—did that have anything to do with Joel?"

"You noticed, huh?" Katie asks, but answers her own question before I can. "Of course. You're an operative. Joel was in the class across from ours, and since they were lined up in the hall alongside us, I plucked him out and showed him a secret hiding place. I told him about the chatter this morning and that he should go there if he had even the slightest worry."

"So Joel knows you're MI6?"

"He thinks I'm the same person I was when I protected him in London—part of a private security team hired by his father. I was undercover and went to school with him. We made sure I was in all of his classes. There have been threats to his family before this one," Katie explains. "Anyway, I sincerely hope he's in that safe room right now, waiting for me to come give him word that it's safe to leave."

"That's why you didn't want me to kill Koval—in case he'd somehow gotten to Joel."

So much is making sense now. I wished she'd trusted me enough to tell me earlier. Maybe I'd have risked going through that stairwell door, even though I'd still have kept her from going.

"I was ninety-nine percent certain Joel was okay, but that one percent was enough to worry me, especially after Marchuk talked about Koval moving packages. I needed to confirm Koval hadn't gotten to Joel first and taken him somewhere I'd never find. But we ran into him in the hall and he grabbed me. Then we got locked out on the roof. Then Berg came—"

"But I slowed you down trying to save Bunker, and then you had to come save us both."

"Of course, I wanted to help you, but I also hoped Koval would be here with Joel. When he wasn't . . . and now that we know about the groundskeeper's tunnel . . ."

Katie doesn't—or can't—finish her thought. I want to do for her what she did for me up on the roof. Make her feel the mission is still viable.

"No, I'm certain Koval hasn't taken him from the building. Joel never showed up in my chem lab and wasn't there when the hostiles invaded. As long as they didn't find out where you told him to hide, Joel should still be here."

"We need to get to the main office," Katie says, heading for the stairs.

I follow her, and Bunker takes that as his cue to rejoin us.

"That's where you're hiding him?" I ask. "The school is swarming with CIA and locals, with the highest concentration of them probably in the office."

"Not *in* the office. Across from it."

"Across from the office is the trophy case," Bunker points out.

"Exactly," Katie says as though that should explain everything.

Carlisle's trophy case is nothing like you'd find in any

other school. For one thing, it takes up nearly the whole wall opposite the office. There are a lot of famous people out there who made their earliest marks on the world while they were at Carlisle, so the case holds not only awards they earned here, but recognition for whatever they did after. We've had two governors, one secretary of defense, an opera singer, so many Nobel prize winners and MacArthur grant recipients that it's embarrassing, and even a couple of Olympic medalists despite Carlisle's fairly sad sports tradition.

"Ah, the trophy case," I say. The case is so big there's an alcove at either end, both with doors to access the back of it. "We should take the stairs that come out on the end farthest from the office. Then it's only a few steps to the alcove."

"Won't it be locked?" Bunker asks.

"There are only two sets of keys as far as I know, and I lifted both from the office earlier this morning. Joel has one and I have the other," Katie explains. "Plus, we always have you. With all those muscles, in a pinch you could probably just knock the door in, right?"

Bunker just starts beaming, but it's hard to tell whether she's for-real flirting with him or spy-flirting. You should never trust anything a spy tells you. We don't always know how to separate truth from truthiness. Still, I do feel a little twinge of jealousy.

Luckily, Berg's team hasn't begun searching the lowest level of the building yet, so we reach the first floor with no problem. Katie is about to open the door to check whether the coast is clear, but Bunker stops her.

"Let me. It's okay if they catch me. If there's a cop right

outside the door, you guys can go back the way you came and let me take one for the team."

Katie puts a hand on his arm and says, "Oh, Bunk-ah. You're so gallant."

Bunker starts grinning until he catches the evil look I'm throwing at him and cracks the door open before closing it again. "So here's the situation. There are two uniforms guarding the office, which now appears to be the command center. I ascertained—"

"Ignore him. He's watched too many bad spy movies," I say, elbowing Bunker out of my way so I can take a look myself. "Their backs are to us. Bunker, you wait here— fewer people to get caught trying to access the trophy case."

"But I can be your lookout," Bunker offers.

"Be our lookout from here," I tell him. "Call me if you see anyone coming."

"I don't want to risk using my walkie-phone and messing anything up since we have the confession on it, and Sveta took my real phone," Bunker says, looking sheepish.

I remove the password lock from my phone and hand it to him. "Call Katie. Her number's in there."

"It is?" Katie asks.

"From before, when we . . . when I thought I might need it again."

Katie smiles at me.

Fortunately, Bunker doesn't protest being left behind, and Katie and I are able to move from the stairwell to the alcove undetected. We both stand in the shadows until she can get the door unlocked. Once inside, Katie turns on her flashlight and I can see that we're in a sort of hallway that runs parallel to the trophy case, a wall on one side, sliding doors to access the case on the other. But it doesn't run the full length of the case. It stops about midway, ending in what looks like a closet, probably accessible from the other alcove in a mirror image. It's a great hiding place.

Except it isn't. When Katie opens the closet door, Joel isn't there.

Now we know what Sveta meant when she said we were too late.

CHAPTER 28

It takes a second for me to process what I see. All this time I'd thought at least one of my friends had escaped this day of terror, but instead of finding Joel, we find Jonesy, bound and gagged. He hadn't gone home with a bad headache before the incursion began. So how did he get here? And has he been here the whole time? But now I know where that roll of duct tape disappeared to. Jones was bound and gagged by his own office supplies.

When I go to remove the gag, Katie stops me.

"How do we know he isn't one of them?"

"Because he's my friend," I say.

"So was I, and you didn't have a clue who I really was."

She has me there, so I step away from Jones, but only for a second. "Whether he's a good guy or bad, we still need him to talk."

Katie rummages around in her purse and pulls out . . . a tube of lipstick. Okay.

"Don't even think about screaming," she says, putting the lipstick near Jonesy's neck. "I have three million volts aimed at your sternocleidomastoid."

Of course Katie has a stun gun. And exceptional knowledge of human anatomy.

"I thought you'd gotten out. How did you get here, all tied up?" I ask Jones as I remove the gag and then immediately step away from him. I'm not as suspicious as Katie, but I'm also not dumb.

"Save the reunion for later," Katie interrupts. "Where's Joel?"

Jones flexes his mouth and jaw muscles, trying to recover from wearing the gag. "Well, that was annoying. Can you untie my hands?" Jones asks. He's so calm about it that I'm wondering if Katie is right.

"No, we cannot." Katie moves the stun gun a hair closer to Jones's sterno-whatever. "Answer the question."

"As you'll recall, Ms. Carmichael, this morning you came by asking to look through the lost-and-found closet. I'd stepped into Ms. Dodson's office while you were allegedly looking for your missing umbrella, but when I returned just ten seconds later, I noticed two sets of keys were missing from the key cabinet, the ones to the trophy case. And so were you. Then during the fire drill, I watched you extract Joel Easter from his class's line and take him to the alcove. I put two and two together—"

"I wanted to show Joel where to hide out in case anything happened. It's *you* who shouldn't be here," Katie says. "And you're the observant one, aren't you? A little *too* observant to just be the office guy, don't you think, Peter?"

I do actually, but I don't want to believe Jonesy is a bad guy since, until now, he was my only other friend at Carlisle. "Finish your story, Jones."

"I'd been sick all morning, hungover—I told you about that, Jake, remember? Anyway, I was in the bathroom when all the announcements began, so I stayed in there, hiding out. Then, when I heard your announcement . . . well, it sounded crazy and I figured a brother couldn't make up some shit like that. So I came here to hide out."

"But I had all the keys."

"Not all," Jones says, smiling a little bit.

We hear the crackling sound of a stun gun being turned on.

I shake my head at Katie and she turns it off.

"Jones, you might want to get to the part about Joel going missing, if you know anything about it."

"I figured whoever was looking for you would sweep the building and check the bathrooms, so I came here." Considering Katie has been threatening to Taser him in a critical section of the circulatory system, Jones is pretty chill in recounting his story. As if he's been rehearsing it. "That's when I found Joel. We thought we'd hide out here until help came, but he came first."

"Who?" Katie asks.

"The janitor."

Koval.

"I swear to God, when we find that guy, we need to end him once and for all," I say.

"And you just let him in?" Katie asks Jones. "Are you kidding me? If Joel is hurt . . . maybe you really are just the office guy if you'd let—"

"I didn't have to let him in. He's the janitor. He had a key. So he says he's looking for a place to hide out, too. He said he saw one of these terrorists coming—"

"Who said anything about them being terrorists? As far as you know, they're bank robbers," Katie asks. "And you certainly know the lingo, don't you? *Sweep* the building and *extract* Joel. Civilians don't talk like that, Peter."

I ignore Katie, even though she's sounding more and more convincing. "Then what happened?"

"The janitor put a choke hold on me. That guy is huge. He could choke hold a grizzly. When I came to, I was bound and they both were gone."

"Sorry, Peter, but I don't buy it," Katie says. "He's probably some kind of decoy. If he were simply Joe Blow office worker, wouldn't Koval have just killed him?"

"Mr. Smith, what's going on?" Jones asks. "Who is she? Who are *you,* for that matter?"

Katie answers before I can. "He's Mr. Smith about as much as you're Mr. Jones. Can't you Americans get a little more creative with the cover names? Here, hold this."

Katie hands me the lipstick stun gun and before I can stop her, she jabs a syringe into Jonesy's arm.

"Again with the tranquilizer? I'm sure Jonesy is a good guy." Well, pretty sure. "Before he knocked out Jones, Koval might have inadvertently dropped a clue to where he was taking Joel. He was trying to tell us—"

"He was wasting our time," Katie explains, "and he's probably one of them."

"A black spy from Ukraine?"

"They *do* have black people in Ukraine, you know. When you were there, you fit in just fine, apparently," Katie reminds me. "But no, I figure him for a hired mercenary, like the one with the New York accent, or the groundskeeper."

Katie is great and everything, but her inability to see

anything but black and white, good and evil, is making me a little crazy. People aren't that easy. I'm a hacker, but even I realize real life isn't so binary. Neither is the spy game.

"I may not have a bottomless bag of spy supplies like you, but one thing I know is people. Jones is a good guy. I trust him."

"Sorry, but I don't. But if you're right, he'll appreciate that we did it to save Joel. Besides, that was the last of my carfentanil, and it was barely a drop. He's probably just asleep, not really unconscious, which means he won't be out for very long, so let's get moving. I just hope Joel is still in the building."

I'm about to follow her, but something stops me.

"Wait. Hear that?" I ask Katie.

"What am I supposed to be hearing?"

"Voices . . ."

"Are they telling you where we can find Joel? Otherwise—"

"Not in my head. Out in the hallway."

"Who is it?"

"Dodson. Berg's team must have located the office staff in the auditorium," I whisper, stepping over Jones and heading out the other side of the closet. "Andrews was guarding them, which means Berg should know by now that she's a dirty cop. If there were only six as we suspected, that just leaves Koval to capture. And his sister."

"Peter," Katie says, following me.

I put a finger to Katie's lips. "Shhh. If we can hear them, they can hear us. They might give us some intel. Maybe Dodson and her staff were kept in the same place as Joel."

Katie must see the logic in this because she stays quiet.

"That's him. That's the one who said he was a detective," Dodson says, and I'm guessing she's pointing out Marchuk, who must still be in the office where we left him unconscious. "The other one was a woman named Andrews. She had a radio, a badge, knew a lot about the area. She was very convincing as a police officer. How was I to know they weren't real?"

"Thank you, ma'am. You and your staff can go with these officers so they can get your official statements. Don't worry," Berg is saying. "They're the real deal."

There is some murmuring of voices I can't decipher, probably the rest of the office staff talking low, still in shock, and then Dodson adds from farther down the hall, "We're still missing one. My assistant's assistant disappeared just before everything happened, and we haven't heard from him. I fear they have him."

"Thank you, Ms. Dodson. We'll find him."

For a moment, I only hear the clicking of Dodson's heels down the hall, and then another male voice asks, "You think the assistant was one of their inside men?" I recognize it as Berg's second-in-command, from up on the roof. I'm beginning to wonder if I'm the only one who doesn't suspect Jonesy, and whether that's a bad idea.

Katie tugs on my shirt sleeve and points at Jones. "We need to get out of here before they start looking for him."

I'm about to follow her back the way we came, but Berg says something that makes me stay.

"I don't know, but the local PD is saying they have one missing, too. This Andrews person was so convincing to the principal because she wasn't pretending. That stupid kid wasn't being paranoid—not about the dirty cop, anyway."

"You think there's some truth in his story about the hacker being on the other side?" the second one asks.

"It may have been a mistake to ignore him. I can't mess this thing up, Hudson. Rogers and I are both up for that promotion, and it's mine if I can show the assistant director how idiotic her nursery-school initiative is. I've got a local uniform watching him. I'll get her to bring him back in here."

There is a thirty-second pause in their conversation, long enough for Berg to radio the officer in charge of me. Then Berg says, "Are you fucking kidding me? I gave you one job: to watch a seventeen-year-old kid."

"I think I just got that cop in trouble," I whisper to Katie.

"In the uniform's defense," Hudson is saying, "the kid's a seventeen-year-old highly trained operative, no matter what you think of Rogers's program. And apparently not bad at it. He neutralized four of six known hostiles and identified one as a rogue cop. What if he's also right about the hacker being responsible for—"

"Shut up, Hudson."

There's a brief silence before Hudson speaks again.

"So . . . new objectives?"

"Objective, singular. Let the locals handle their dirty cop. Find that goddamn kid."

CHAPTER 29

I'm kinda surprised when we return to find Bunker right where we left him. But I'm glad to find he not only hasn't been captured, but he's looking a lot less green than he did in the basement.

"Where's Joel?" he asks.

"Koval got to him first," Katie explains. "We don't even know if they're still in the building. Wherever they are, we need to find them before Koval can leave town. Or the country. I don't even want to think about what he might do to Joel."

"Yeah, but we'd better be armed with more than a couple of screwdrivers and a Sharpie, which is all I got."

Bunker starts smiling, so I know he's been up to something. "Well, I can help with that. While you guys were gone, I did a little intel-gathering of my own."

"Oh, jeez, what did you do, Bunk?"

"Called your boss. Or who I figured was your boss, because it was the last number you dialed and it had a 202 area code—I've memorized all the area codes," he adds for Katie's benefit. For some reason, his father thought it was important to take a phone book into the bomb shelter

with him. Maybe he didn't think they'd be in there for fifteen years. Not only had Bunker memorized all the area
codes, but he can tell you the address of everyone in
Tucumcari, New Mexico, up to Richard Beckman, at least
as of 1999.

"Um, why?" I ask, afraid to hear the reason.

"Figured while I waited for you guys to come back, I
could get some information about this Koval person."

"And how did that go?" I ask, afraid to hear the answer.

"First she yelled at me for having your phone. Then she
yelled about you giving me your phone. Then she interrogated me, asking questions only my dad and I should
know, to make sure I was who I said I was. And what's up
with those questions? Don't ever call my dad paranoid
again, because clearly Big Brother has been watching."

"So what did she *say,* Bunker?" Katie asks, not especially
interested in Bunk's fears about government overreach.

One day I'll have to explain to him that the minute he
became my friend, Rogers probably opened a file on him
and his father.

"I expect her to call back any minute," Bunker says just
as his phone vibrates.

Or *my* phone, and he's about to answer it.

"Give me that," I say, grabbing it from him.

"You're really onto something here," Rogers says when
I answer. "Your friend caught me up on what you know
so far—and, by the way, we'll need to have a long chat
about that. Giving him your phone will definitely be a
problem for your next performance review."

"But boss—"

"I said later, Smith. Let's deal with the bigger problem

right now. There has been chatter for weeks now that
Vadim Koval has been planning a hostile takeover of
Marchuk's arms trade while also proving to the terrorist
world that he can provide even better service than the old
man did. I've got some people gathering more intel. We
should have a report for Berg in the next half hour. You
need to bring him in on this, Smith," Rogers warns. "Don't
try doing this by yourself."

"Not that Berg would ever listen to me, but I don't need
his help. But no worries. I have backup."

"Smith, I'm warning—"

"Sorry, boss. Gotta go."

After I hang up, I relay the intel to Bunker and Katie.

"I'm calling MI6 if your Berg won't help us find Joel,"
she says, taking out her phone. "We need officers at every
airport in the metro area, every train station, roadblocks
on every road out of this state."

"Hold on, Katie. Y'all can't run operations on our soil.
At least not overt ones, and all of that sounds pretty overt
to me."

My phone starts vibrating again. It's the third call since
I hung up on Rogers. She is so going to kill me.

"Not so fast," says a woman's voice on the stairs above us.

Uh oh. Rogers is going to have to wait in line.

It's Andrews, and she looks like she wants to kill someone. Or three someones. I need to think of a way out of this
on the quick.

"We've been busted," Bunker says. "I guess my spy days
are over."

"Wow. This is one busy stairwell. You'd think Berg would
have checked it out, with it being just down the hall from

his command center," I say, a little more loudly than necessary. "And Bunk, I'm guessing *all* your days are over if it's up to her. Don't believe the uniform. She's no more a good guy than her partner Marchuk is."

"Hands out of your pockets. Slowly," she orders, pointing her gun at me. I comply.

She doesn't have to ask Bunker, whose face has gone back to a shade of about-to-puke green. He already has his arms raised, though I'm worried he might faint any second. Katie doesn't look sick at all. She looks like she's thinking about charging Andrews and killing her with her bare hands.

Which is why Andrews turns the gun on Katie. "And you. Did I just hear you say you were MI6? What the hell is the world coming to? They're hiring officers who haven't even finished their growth spurts, but *I* apply for the FBI, DHS, *and* CIA, and not a single one will take me."

"Uh, because you're a dirty cop?" I offer, hoping to distract Andrews for a minute by getting her to talk about herself. It worked on Sveta, except Katie won't be crashing through the ceiling. "I'm pretty sure that silencer attachment on your pistol isn't standard issue from the police department's gun vault. Police—at least not good cops—don't use silencers."

"*They* didn't know I was dirty. And I didn't go to the other side until after they rejected me. I got sick of playing by the good ol' boys' rules."

"So you turned traitor to your country because you were rejected by some *boys*?" Katie asks. "You should be kicked out of the girl club now."

"Please. That's all you are—a girl. I've been a cop longer than you've been alive. The struggle is real for a sister in uniform. *Still* in uniform, *still* working a beat. Passed up for promotions by—"

"Better cops than you?" I say.

"If you know I'm MI6, then you know what I'm capable of," Katie says, taking the smallest step toward Andrews.

"Better back up, little girl. You may be a spy, but bullets can still stop MI6 agents just as well as they can stop a CIA officer. Or a sickly-looking redhead," Andrews says as she points her weapon first at Katie, then me, then Bunker.

"Look, I need to find Koval. I didn't ruin my career just to go to jail. You know what they do to cops in jail? I want the money I was guaranteed, and the passport, and a way out of here like he promised me."

"Wait. You double-crossed Marchuk, too? Was anyone loyal to that guy?" I ask, stalling until the help I hope is on the way gets here. "But I feel you on that dude. I remember when I was in Ukraine—"

Andrews aims her gun in my direction.

"Shut up," Andrews says. "You talk too much. And too loud. Only thing I need from you is to find Koval for me. It sounded to me like you were working on a plan, super-spies."

"And if we help you, then what?" I ask.

"And then I'll get the hell out of the country and enjoy an early retirement."

"You don't need Bunker for that. I mean, look at the poor guy." Katie's right—I'm pretty sure Bunker's about to hurl any second. "Let him go or I won't help you."

"You make a good point. One superspy is probably just as good as two, and a helluva lot easier to keep my eye on," Andrews says, coming down one more step toward us and taking aim at Katie. "I'll take Smith with me, but kill the two of you."

That's when the doors burst open, filling the stairwell with SWAT officers from behind and above us.

CHAPTER 30

Well, it's about damn time.

"We had to get in position," Berg says to me.

My expression must be talking for me, but I let him know in words what I think. "It took you long enough. I was running out of ways to stall her."

Katie looks over at me and asks, "You—but how?"

"My boss has been blowing up my phone ever since I hung up on her. I answered her last call but didn't say anything, just left an open line."

"Man, I was wondering how you were going to get us out of that one," Bunker says, probably taking his first breath since Andrews said she was going to kill him. He looks like he might pass out.

Katie smiles. "So that whole thing about the busy stairwell being near the office was just letting her know where we were. Not bad for just a hacker."

"Well, I figured I owed you one," I say, feeling damned good about myself. Yup, I'll admit it. "Now we're even."

"Well, not that I was counting, but you *still* owe me one."

She winks at me and I don't think she's just talking

about our bad guy count. I swear to God if Berg wasn't here and several SWAT officers weren't trying to subdue Andrews—who is putting up one helluva fight—I'd kiss Katie right now.

"Oh, young love. How sweet," Berg says in a tone that makes it clear he doesn't find it sweet at all. "At least act like you're operatives."

"Operatives, plural?" Katie asks.

"Drop the act. I know who you are. I've spoken to your boss. And if we're keeping score, I just saved both your asses."

"Only with their help," Bunker says. "Every perp you have in custody, we wrapped up for you."

"Who is he?" Berg asks. "Another baby operative?"

"I've been deputized by Peter Smith into the Company. Caesar Augustus Octavian Murphy, at your service, sir."

"*That's* your real first name? And second? And third?" I ask Bunker, trying to suppress a laugh.

"Totally suits me, right?"

Not. At. All.

But what I tell him is, "Absolutely. But you know the third name is kind of overkill. Caesar, Augustus, and Octavian were the same person."

"My father was really into the Roman Empire. Talk about your government spies."

"We don't need your family history, just your official statement. Hudson, take Caesar away," Berg says to his second officer.

That starts me laughing because one, it's funny, and two, if I don't laugh I just might lose it after what I've been through. Berg apparently doesn't find Bunker's name or the situation as amusing as I do. He grabs me by the arm and practically drags me out of the stairwell, across the hall, and into the office. That cures me of the giggles real quick.

I pull my arm from his grip. "If you care about your health, you best stop manhandling me."

"You'd have to actually be a man for me to do that," Berg says, apparently in search of an ass-kicking. Forget the CIA training. I grew up on the streets of Southside Atlanta, where they also teach combat skills. After the day I've had, I'm about ready to demonstrate them.

"Oh, so you're calling me a boy, now?"

"I'm calling you under arrest. You and your girlfriend, at least until her government gets here to take her off my hands," Berg says, and no matter how controlled he's keeping his voice, I see in his eyes that he's actually worried I might go off on him, which is enough for me. I get it together long enough to regain my focus, which should be on finding Joel.

"I don't think so. Peter and I have a mission to complete," Katie says.

"Rogers will back me on that, Berg. Do yourself a favor and instead of blocking us, help us out. You're always looking for a promotion, and this is the kind of mission that'll get you one."

But Berg isn't trying to hear anything I have to say, and instead calls over a couple of uniforms.

"Escort this one home," he says, pointing at Bunker. "Take these two to lockup. And don't let the kid get away this time, or I'll—"

"You aren't taking him anywhere," says a familiar voice from behind me.

It's Jones, standing in the doorway and looking hella groggy, thanks to Katie's drugs. Deep down, I never really suspected Jonesy was on the wrong side, and I totally appreciate the effort, but he must still be out of it if he thinks the school office guy outranks Berg and his team, all of whom have just pulled their sidearms and aimed them at him.

"See? I told you I didn't give him that much carfentanil," Katie says. "But it must have been enough to make him delusional."

"And who the hell are you?" Berg asks.

"Tell your men to stand down," I say. "He's Dodson's receptionist, the one she told you went missing."

"Oh, I see. We should stand down just because he's a Carlisle employee, like the groundskeeper and the janitor."

Okay, so Berg has a point, but I know he *and* Katie are wrong about Jonesy.

Jones smiles and shakes his head a little, like he knows what's up and it's the rest of us who are clueless.

"No, I'm not a Carlisle employee. In fact, you and I have the same employer, Berg—at least at the top level," Jones says, starting to sound as crazy as I must have a few minutes ago when I almost lost it on Berg. "I'm Special Agent Richardson, FBI."

Um, what?

"Do you have credentials on you?" Berg asks, scowling and apparently as skeptical as I am.

"I'm undercover, so of course not. Call your assistant director. He'll verify."

Berg gestures to Hudson, who gets on the phone.

"In the meantime, I'll be taking Officer Smith with me for a debriefing. You don't have any problem with that, do you, Smith?"

"Uh . . . no?"

"And I'm going with," Katie says.

"Like hell you're taking him anywhere," Berg says to Jones, ignoring both Katie and me. "Even if you're who you say you are, they're mine to debrief. At least the boy is. I don't care about the girl, but he's CIA."

I can't seem to come to my own defense because I'm still too dumbstruck by the fact that mild-mannered Jonesy has been an undercover agent all this time. From now on, I will never trust anyone with the last name of Jones or Smith to be who they claim to be. And also, Katie is right. We really need to get more creative with our cover names.

"He's who he says he is, chief," Hudson says once he gets off the phone.

As if to confirm what Hudson has just told us, though I still don't quite believe it, an FBI agent enters the office, followed by Hudson, and hands Jones a badge, tactical holster, and two handguns.

"Where did he come from? Who let your man in here?" Berg asks. "I didn't call the FBI in on this."

Hudson says, "He had credentials, sir. I had to let him in."

"He sure did. This is a domestic matter now. You know it's in violation of CIA rules to conduct missions on US soil," Jones says, giving me a stern look. "Besides, I thought Smith has been nothing but a thorn in your side. Seems you'd *want* me to take him off your hands."

"Yeah, that's what it seems like, Berg." I finally manage to say something, but it's so weak, it probably would have been best to remain quiet.

"You only want him because you figured out Peter's a better operative than you'll ever be," Katie says, getting all up in Berg's face. "He's pretty much handed this operation over to you with a bow on it: Marchuk and crew, Andrews. No more freebies for you. Let's go, Agent Richardson."

"Sorry, Ms. Carmichael, but you nearly stunned me and *did* sedate me. Why would I take you anywhere with me?"

"Because I am here on request of Her Majesty's secret service. And I—"

"Like I said, Ms. Carmichael, this is a domestic matter and I'm certainly not working with a foreign spy," Jones explains. "I only need Smith for a debriefing."

Katie turns to Jones and gives him such a look that I think every last one of us in the room is afraid. "This was my mission long before any of you even knew who Joel Easter was. I am not about to let—"

"Who's Joel Easter?" Berg makes the mistake of interrupting her again.

"See, now it's your turn to shut up, Berg," Katie says before turning to Jones. "If you think for one minute you're kicking me off this mission, be prepared to feel the wrath of the British Secret Service *and* the Prime Minister, because—"

Jones looks at her like he just figured out that despite the plaid skirt and saddle shoes, the Katie standing before him is not the one who won homecoming queen.

"Okay, okay, my mistake," Jones says wisely. "You come, too."

"And me?" Bunker asks.

"You aren't working undercover with Interpol or the Defense Intelligence Agency, are you?" Jones asks.

"No, but—"

"Sorry, no civilians," Jones says, cutting Bunker off. "And now time is critical, so we need to go."

Bunker looks disappointed, but goes with a local officer to give his statement as Jones instructs. I don't know if I'll see him again, since that's how it works with the Company sometimes, so before he leaves, I tell him, "Thanks for having my back."

"Always, brother."

He gives me a man-hug and this time I don't care who's there, so I give him a real hug back before the officer takes him away.

CHAPTER 31

So what's the plan?" Katie asks Jones once we're away from Berg and his people. "I think the way to go is to split up—you search inside, Peter and I will start searching the grounds—find and secure Joel, then eliminate Koval."

"I know you want to find Joel, but we need to reassess the situation first, and from there, figure out where Koval might have taken him," Jones says, but he doesn't know Katie. So much of espionage is watching and waiting, so I'm not sure how she passed all the psych evals for the job, because her patience level is always set to low.

"Can we do it on the fly? Every minute we spend talking about finding Joel is time we aren't actually finding him."

"She's more a doer than a planner," I explain to Jones. "But he's got a point, Katie. This is probably not the time to just wing it."

Katie sighs but follows us into the nearest unoccupied classroom. "Okay, so reassess, regroup, whatever, and let me know when you're both ready to actually *do* something. I'll be over here reassessing and regrouping my supplies."

She stakes out the teacher's desk at the front of the room, where she dumps out the contents of her bag. Jones takes a seat in the front row and I pace the empty space between them. Pacing always helps me think better.

"All right, Smith, give me a quick recap."

I start with the storming of my chem lab, the naming of all the characters, the roles they played, and end with where we stand now.

"And now Vadim Koval has Joel, in case you forgot," Katie says as she breaks into parts what had been a small flute. Soccer, engineering club, spy. How did she find time for band, too, and why didn't I know about it? "We should be out there searching instead of in here talking, guys."

I go over to the window and watch the arrival of frantic parents. It's strange that a couple of hours ago, all the chaos was inside and I longed for the peace beyond Carlisle's walls. Now it's the opposite—law enforcement agents are calmly and methodically going about their work inside, while the rest of the city is trying not to lose it outside as word of the incursion reaches them.

"Maybe Sveta can tell us where Koval's keeping him."

I remind Katie, "She's unconscious, thanks to your needles of doom."

"I have ways of bringing her back."

I don't doubt she carries some kind of carfentanil antidote in that bag, because now she's holding up a small pistol made from the reassembled parts of her flute—I'm guessing a .22 caliber, from the size of it. But probably not. I've only known her as a spy for a little over an hour, but I can't see Katie carrying such a wimpy caliber gun, even if it was made out of a band instrument.

"The only reason Koval wants Joel is to get to his father. I have a man at the federal lab guarding him. Let me call and fill him in, in case Koval has tried to make contact with Joel's dad," Jones says, dialing a number.

"That's hopeful," I tell Katie. "Koval needs Joel alive and well, and close by, until he can use him as leverage. And he can't get to the father if the FBI is guarding him."

"Hmm, my agent isn't answering."

He makes a second phone call and though we can't hear the other end of it, it's obvious from his expression that it's bad news. When he hangs up, he fills us in.

"I called his desk at the lab and got his supervisor, who says Nolan Easter and his guest left for lunch and never returned."

"What guest?" I ask.

"My agent posed as a visiting scientist. He and Mr. Easter left for lunch over two hours ago."

"That's a long lunch, especially when your agent knows there's intel suggesting possible trouble today. Maybe he took Joel's dad somewhere safer," I say, more for Katie's nerves than because I believe it.

"Not many places in town safer than a secured federal lab," Jones says.

"The police department," I offer.

"No, my agent would have called me."

"Are you certain your agent isn't on Marchuk's payroll like Andrews?" Katie asks.

"I trust him," Jones says as he rests one hand on top of his head. "Maybe Marchuk has more men in town, and they intercepted my agent somehow."

"Uh oh," I say, flashing back to the visitor's sign-in screen.

"Jones, did you take your lunch the same time you always do during fifth period?"

"Yes, and I hate the idea that you've been spying on me this whole time."

"Not spying. Intel-gathering," I say. "So whoever fills in for you while you're at lunch must have been at the window when he arrived."

"When *who* arrived?" Jones asks.

"Mr. Easter, just before the end of fifth period and the lunch bell. It didn't occur to me until you said his full name because he signed in as Dr. Nolan E.," I explain.

"Could they have been here this whole time?" Katie asks. "Where? And doing what?"

"He gave the purpose for the visit as a *parent-teacher conference*. Guess who the teacher was."

"Maitland," Katie says. "So he wasn't wandering the halls for no reason when Bunker found him in the biology lab. He's somehow in on all of this."

"The guy was always my least favorite teacher," Jones says, "but to be involved in this? I don't know. Where's the motive?"

"I was so busy scoping out new students as suspects, I didn't even consider new employees like you, Jones, or Maitland. He arrived this year too, with a gambling problem which is apparently a lot worse than I thought."

"That's a classic motive. Could be he was in debt to dangerous people, and Marchuk offered him a big payout. But what would Marchuk have paid him to do?" Jones asks.

"Joel was in fifth-period World Geo," Katie says. "They probably planned to lift him then, with Maitland's help.

Something must have scared him into the trophy case before Maitland could deliver him. When they couldn't find Joel in World Geo or at lunch, they had to go to plan B and take him out of sixth-period chem."

"Where they knew I'd be," I say, finishing her thought. "They anticipated I'd fight back and came in through the ceiling for the element of surprise, only to find neither of us there."

"So they've been hunting Smith only because they thought you and Joel were together, or that you had hidden him away somewhere," Jones says.

"Oh no, Marchuk definitely wanted to kill me. He was just shortsighted in personally seeing to it while Koval ran the more critical operation. If Marchuk's awake, he's sitting in a room being interrogated right now, and still probably doesn't realize Koval took over his plan."

"Which is what, exactly?" Katie asks.

"They couldn't just stroll into NIST, especially with Jones's guy on the premises."

"I told you, the agent was undercover as a scientist," Jones offers.

"Yeah, there's a reason for the CIA. Y'all just aren't as good at subterfuge as we are. Sorry, Jones, but someone on Marchuk's team saw right through his cover, made your guy for a cop, and intercepted him like you said. Or Easter managed to ditch your agent during lunch. Either way, he didn't get the job done."

Jones doesn't look too pleased with my assessment, but gets on his phone and hurriedly tells someone to be on the lookout for a possible missing agent.

"Might you two chest-pound some other time, Peter?"

Katie asks when Jones finishes his call, her already-thin patience nearly worn out.

"Right. So they must have planned Carlisle as the drop point for Mr. Easter to deliver his encryption software. No one would think anything of him visiting the school, and having Joel wrapped up here in World Geo, they had leverage to make sure his dad delivered. They never expected Maitland would screw up his part of the plan. All he had to do was take Joel to wherever Koval was holding his dad."

"I bet Maitland did something to scare Joel into asking for a hall pass and never coming back," Katie says.

"Probably," I say, recalling how nervous Maitland was about handing over his laptop to me. Now I wish I'd let him tell me why he needed it so badly. He wouldn't have told me the truth, but his lie might have been a clue.

"So Mr. Easter was supposed to bring his encryption data to Carlisle, Koval hands over Joel," Jones says.

"Except he won't. We all know they never hand over the collateral."

We're all worried, but Katie sounds and looks like she's way past that point. I guess after guarding Joel in England, he has become more than just a mission for her. I don't want her going on tilt thinking how Koval won't be freeing Joel, so I pretend I didn't hear what she said and focus on the mission.

"It wasn't as simple as that. I'm guessing Easter signed in and out at the same time. He wanted it to appear as though he'd come and gone, when really he remained in the building."

"But why not just hand over the flash drive or whatever and get out? Why hang around?" Katie asks.

"Maybe at the last minute Easter had second thoughts on handing it over," Jones says.

"No, not when his kid's life is at stake," I say.

I remember what Marchuk said in the office, that Koval was "making sure package is secure until *other* package arrives safely." Joel must have been the first package. But Dr. Easter was already in the building by then, so he couldn't have been the second package Marchuk was waiting on to arrive.

"I think he had to do some work on his code before he could hand it off to Marchuk. He couldn't just download all the algorithms and cyphers onto a flash drive and walk out of NIST without cybersecurity noticing," I explain. "He probably had to copy off bits and pieces of the code to keep from raising attention from security, and then brought them here to assemble it back together. I'm not an expert on the cryptography side of hacking, but I'm certain reassembling the code takes more than a minute."

Marchuk was waiting on the "arrival" of the reassembled code.

"Berg's team was in position while we were in that hallway dealing with Koval. No way could Koval and Easter have gotten past the perimeter Berg set up," Katie says, sounding hopeful for the first time since we discovered Jones behind the trophy case instead of Joel. "They're still here."

Jones must be hopeful, too, because he almost smiles. Or maybe he's impressed by just how good a couple of seventeen-year-old operatives are.

"Let me get some backup and also make sure we take that teacher into custody. I'll be right back."

The second Jones leaves the room, Katie says, "I bet they went to Maitland's office to put the code back together."

"You're probably right, though Koval would be taking a risk with CIA sweeping the building. They may have moved. Maitland's office is kind of out of the way though, maybe they haven't gotten to it yet," I say, before I realize where this is going. "Hold on, Katie. You heard Jones—we need backup, you're a foreign operative—"

"You're crazy if you think I'm waiting. Jones will catch up," Katie says. "Follow me or don't, but I'm going to save Joel."

CHAPTER 32

When we get to Maitland's office, it's locked.

"That's probably a good sign they're still in there. I've been in Maitland's office and his desk is off to the right. I'm good at picking locks, so if we can sneak in and surprise them, we'll—"

Katie just kicks the door in. But she shouldn't have.

Nolan Easter is on a laptop, busy giving terrorists access to our nuclear codes; Joel is looking dazed and confused, as though he still can't believe any of this is happening; and Koval's standing there with a gun on both of them. It's a helluva lot bigger than that rinky-dink flute thing Katie's holding.

"Let him go, Koval," Katie demands. "Take his dad if you want, but let Joel go."

Her patience skills are weak, but I'd give her an A for bravery. Koval's response is just what I expect—he laughs at Katie and her gun, which looks like it came from Toys "R" Us.

"Surely you don't expect me to do that. What leverage would I have then?" Koval asks. "Besides, we're almost done here—right, Easter?"

"Look, Koval, you have no chance of getting out of this

building," I warn him. "Jones is already pissed about you knocking him out, and now he's on his way with reinforcements."

Koval keeps the gun on the Easters but he watches Katie and me for our reaction. His expression is a mix of sinister and joyful expectation, something I've seen before in people who get their kicks tormenting others. As though this whole ordeal could be as much about pleasure as it is about business.

"Perhaps, but he doesn't know exactly where you are. Before he left for those reinforcements, you didn't tell him you'd be coming to Maitland's office."

"You have mics on us?"

Koval just vaporized the confidence I felt when breaking down his mission for Jones a minute ago. Just when I think I've got a handle on this spy business, these guys one-up me. When could he have possibly dropped a bug on me? I checked the clothes I'm wearing when I took them off the hostile.

He smirks and says, "On Jones. I planted it after I knocked him out and took the boy from the trophy case."

Katie takes a step forward, her gun held straight out in front of her. I attempt to diffuse her move by trying to reason with Koval, hoping I've read him wrong.

"That's right. You only knocked him out. You didn't kill him, though you could have. You didn't hurt Rachel or Katie when you found them in the hall, even though you suspected her."

Koval grabs Joel's hand and raises it where Katie and I can see. "Do not question my ability to hurt him or anyone else."

Okay, so maybe reasoning was the wrong tactic with this guy.

"Look, Koval, you don't really want to hurt a civilian, a kid—"

I'm cut off by Joel's scream piercing the room as Koval crushes his hand inside his own bear-sized paw.

Katie fires her gun. It has zero effect on Koval. He's still standing there looking scared, then surprised, then amused. But me? I can't seem to stay upright.

I feel myself falling and can't do anything about it. I don't hear anything except the sound of people running from the room, and then nothing.

When I come to for the second time today, Jones is standing over me.

"What the hell just happened?"

It feels like I've been out for days, but the clock on Maitland's wall tells me it has only been a few minutes, which is plenty enough time for Koval to have hurt Joel even more than he already has. And if Mr. Easter finished the reassembly job, a few minutes is more than enough time for both Easters to be dead. I need to go find them before time runs out, but I can't even stand up.

Beside me, Katie also tries to stand, but Jones has to catch her as she loses her balance.

"I must have put the flute together wrong and it back-fired."

"Then you'd be dead, unless that wasn't a gun you fired," I say, already suspecting it wasn't, considering this is Katie.

"It doesn't shoot bullets. It was supposed to shoot

nerve gas to render Koval unconscious, but I must have assembled the flute wrong and it got us instead."

"So where are they now?" Jones asks.

"I don't know," Katie says, "but Joel needs a doctor. That beast probably broke every bone in his hand. Hopefully, he hasn't done anything worse. Yet."

Jones instructs the two agents he brought as backup to go find Koval before he says, "You two also need a doctor. I'm calling an EMT, and you're sitting out the rest of the mission."

"No. Absolutely not. The effects of the gas wear off quickly." Katie not only gets to her feet to prove it, she leaves the office, and this time it's our turn to follow her. "And Koval's on the run."

"I don't think he'd leave without his sister. Wait a minute. Jones, did you know you're mic'd up?"

"Yeah, I figured it out on the way back here. It's gone now."

"She probably told him she planned to ambush and kill me in the basement," I continue. "Koval obviously knows that didn't work out well for her. If he left with them, it's either because Dr. Easter didn't finish putting the code back together, he needs them as hostages to safely leave campus, or both. Sveta probably knows where he'd go."

"We might even find him with her," Jones says. "I assume you gave Sveta more of that tranquilizer than you gave me, so she's probably still unconscious."

"I'm going to wake her up with a shot of opioid antagonist to reverse the effects of the tranquilizer, and then I'm going to make her wish I hadn't."

Yeeeah. Katie is a little scary.

When we reach the sub-basement, Sveta is gone. I shouldn't have expected any different. All day, it's been one step forward for the bad guys, two steps back for us.

"How is that even possible? I checked her pulse before we left her and her heart rate had already begun to slow," Katie says. "And even if she came to, Houdini couldn't have escaped the ties I put on her."

"You think Berg got to her first?" Jones asks.

"No, we'd have heard it on the radio." Katie holds up a Motorola. She must notice the incredulous look on my face because she adds, "I snagged it from a desk in the office while Agent Jones was setting that cretin straight."

"Well, I know that cretin, and he is not very discreet," I say, "at least not when it comes to bragging about himself. Believe me, if Berg had found Sveta or her brother, he'd be patting himself on the back about it all over that radio."

"Damn it!" Jones yells, the first time I've ever seen him lose his cool. "Koval got here first."

"That would mean he's moving around with three people now," I say, because it seems so unlikely. "He knows we're after him, assumes Berg and his team are. Four people make for an easy target. Koval would never be so obvious."

Jones draws his weapon as we all realize there's a good chance Koval is still down here somewhere, hiding in the shadows. He hands me the backup revolver from his ankle holster, then nods and hand-signals our directives. Katie and I go the opposite direction of Jones. Thirty seconds later, we all return to the center of the room, having found nothing.

"I still can't see Koval trying to move around with Sveta and two hostages," Katie says. "What are you doing?"

I look up at her for a second before staring at the floor again, walking slowly across the room. "Looking around for a trap door in the floor, like we found in the shed and the janitor's office. Y'all could help, you know."

"But we're in the sub-basement. It seems unlikely, especially in Colorado. Isn't there a lot of rock near the surface?" Katie says.

"Good point, but I'm desperate here." I look overhead. "The ceilings, maybe?"

"They're pretty high. You'd need a ladder, and I don't see a ladder anywhere," Jones says, being about as helpful as Katie.

"Okaaay . . . let's check the walls, then. There's a camera in the hallway outside the door, and Sveta had to assume Berg's team was watching the monitors," I say, beginning to pace between them. "There are no windows, and yet she's gone. I suppose she could have turned off the cameras. She did have a smartwatch. But Berg probably turned off her connectivity, so—"

That's when I notice there's a partial handprint on the dusty shelf I'm standing next to. I can tell by the thick layer of dust on the floor that the shelf had been here a long time, undisturbed, until today. Someone tried to move the shelf back to its original position, but didn't quite make it. I swing one side of the shelf out a few inches from the wall.

"What did you find?" Katie asks.

"I don't know yet, but at some point recently, someone moved this shelf."

Jones takes the other end of the shelf and we move it a couple of feet away from the wall. I run my hand over it and realize it isn't a wall at all.

"There's a draft," I say.

"Hidden door?" Katie asks, and feels for the draft before pushing her shoulder against one side of the door.

It works like a lever and opens the side near me. Inside, we find a safe room that definitely wasn't part of the blueprints I'd memorized.

And inside the safe room are Joel and his father.

People outside the building can probably hear us all sigh in relief.

But that feeling doesn't last long.

As soon as I remove the tape from Mr. Easter's mouth, he says, "You're too late. He already has the flash drive with all my research on it. I'm sorry, but I had to save my son. You saw what he did to Joel's hand. He would have killed us."

Though I never needed to, I've been willing to kill before—for survival, or to complete a mission—but I never *wanted* to. Until now. Koval had better hope I'm not the first one to find him.

"And the hacker—a blond girl—was with him?" I ask.

"We saw her, but she didn't come inside the safe room with us. It was only him," Joel answers after Jones removes his duct-tape gag.

"That makes sense. Someone had to move the shelf back into position after Koval took you two inside with him. And it was too heavy for her to get it back in the exact right position."

"Or she was in a hurry and didn't care about making it look perfect," Jones says.

"Now that I think about it, she wouldn't have cared if Berg caught her on the stairwell camera. He doesn't know she's the hacker, who he thinks is in London somewhere. Berg won't be looking for her. She can just walk right out the door past his guards, the last straggler student to evacuate," I say.

"So Sveta is in the wind, too," Katie says.

Joel's father says, "I think he intended to take us with him as hostages, but changed his mind once we got in here. Maybe he figured we'd slow him down. The only reason my son isn't dead . . ." He doesn't finish the sentence, probably overwhelmed by the thought of it.

"Is because he heard you outside the door, moving the shelf, and got scared," Joel says, finishing his father's thought. He points to another door in the safe room opposite the one we entered. "He took off running through there."

"With the encryption technology that protects us from launching a nuclear strike," I say, the enormity of it sinking in.

Mr. Easter regains his composure and adds, "It must lead to a tunnel of some sort. Perhaps you can still catch him."

When Mr. Easter says *tunnel,* it reminds me of something. Maybe we aren't down for the count just yet.

"Jones, when I was on the roof, I remember seeing an old shed. I thought it was odd because it was too far away from the school to be of any use. If there are passageways down here, maybe that's where it comes out above ground. And if I remember right, it's just outside Berg's perimeter."

"Smith, I like the way you think," Jones says. "I'll try to reach the shed first and head him off above ground. You and Carmichael take the tunnel. Maybe you can catch up to him."

It sounds like a good plan to me, but Katie doesn't respond. In fact, she has been unusually quiet. When we look up to get Katie's confirmation, she is gone.

CHAPTER 33

The tunnel is dark and I can't see a thing, but at least it was built by professionals—it's not one of the groundkeeper's makeshift dirt tunnels. All kinds of fear are running through me right now—fear of being ambushed by Koval, of him unleashing Armageddon on the world, of losing Katie—but at least I don't have to worry about the walls closing in on me—literally. I can stand at full height, which means I can move quickly—or I could if only I could see a damn thing.

Katie has her flashlight, but she must already be too far ahead for me to see it. Or maybe she decided against using it. All I have is my phone. The choice is between using it so I can see where I'm going—along with whoever might be waiting there for me—or stumbling around in total darkness. I assume Koval is trying to get the hell out and didn't hang around in order to capture me, so I go with option one. My flashlight app isn't great, but at least now I'm able to see whether the tunnel just goes straight ahead or has right angles, which would also explain why I can't see the beam of Katie's light.

She can't be more than thirty seconds ahead of me,

but so far, there are no signs of her. I want to call out her name, but that would broadcast to Koval that she's on his tail. About ten yards into the tunnel, I come to a four-way stop. I figured it might happen, but it might as well be a brick wall.

Come on Jake, no freaking out. Choose one.

But choosing the wrong tunnel will cost me time. Plus, there are no markings to distinguish one tunnel from the others, so if I have to backtrack and I'm not careful, I might screw up and disorient myself.

Duh, Jake.

I pull the Sharpie from my pocket and draw an arrow on the floor pointing behind me, toward the safe room, a way out if the other three tunnels turn out to be dead ends.

Just as I'm about to choose a path, I hear something. Since I don't know if the something is good or bad, I can't call out. Using my flashlight is also a bad idea, so I make it go dark. The pitch blackness clears my thoughts, and I realize the sound can only be bad. Katie knew I would follow her. If she'd caught Koval and heard me coming, or if she'd seen the light from my phone, she would call out to me. At the very least, her flashlight would be shining.

Being in the dark also forces me to sharpen my other senses. I'm still standing at the intersection of the four tunnels. They're close. I'd have heard their footsteps if they had moved on. I know they aren't in the tunnel behind me, so I turn to my left, count off five paces, arms outstretched, and stop just inside the first tunnel. I hear nothing. Smell nothing. I walk backwards five paces, which should put me back in the center of the intersection. Then I turn right, and do the same thing in the second tunnel, the one I'd have taken in the first place had I just gone straight ahead. Again, I hear and smell nothing.

One tunnel left. Like my mind is on a delay, I realize the sound was familiar—a jangling of keys, but muted, as though Koval has put the keychain in his pocket rather than wearing it on his belt loop. In this final tunnel, I do the same thing, stepping just inside it. I don't hear anything, but smell strawberries and creosote.

Katie smelled of both those things, but if she was here alone, she'd have called my name by now. If she'd taken down Koval, she'd be talking smack about how she bagged the bad guy first.

So they're both close, except the bad guy has bagged her.

It feels like everything inside me drops at the same time: my stomach, my nerve, my heart. But I keep it together because that madman has Katie.

I step back as silently as I can, hoping Koval doesn't have a dog-boy olfactory sense like I do. I need just a couple of seconds to think how this will play out in a way that doesn't get Katie or me killed. The element of surprise would be great, but he must have seen my flashlight. Koval must assume I followed Katie. He knows I'm close. Probably knows what Katie means to me, so he has that advantage.

But where we both have a level playing ground is the pitch blackness. Except he's been in the tunnels at least a minute longer, and without light longer. Less than a minute has passed since I had my phone on. My pupils have dilated, but not as much as his. Bright light will be more his enemy than mine.

"I know you're there, kid," Koval says, confirming my theories.

I guess he's grown tired of waiting for me to make my move. I have to make one soon, because each second I don't means losing the advantage of less sensitivity to light. But what if the move I make is the wrong one? Fear of getting it wrong nearly paralyzes me.

"And you know I have your girl."

These are the words I need to kick me into gear, and they are enough sound from Koval that I can judge how close he is to me: just a few feet ahead in the tunnel and slightly to my left.

"Come out, come out, wherever you are."

Koval thinks he has the advantage. Any other day, it would be true. He has more experience. He has no compassion. He has my girl.

But that last thing is what wills me to stop him. I raise my gun, ready to shoot in the direction just below his center of gravity. I need to already have my aim as close to the target as possible because I'll only have a few seconds. But Katie is probably positioned in front of him, as a shield. Now I can hear her breathing. It isn't elevated, but regular.

"Get out of here, Peter, while you can!"

Katie's words confirm that she is being restrained, but she has all her senses about her, too.

"What are you waiting for?" Koval singsongs the words like we're playing a game.

One last surge of doubt rises in my gut, trying to immobilize me, but I push it down with a single thought: *If I don't act, Katie will die.*

I hold up my phone with my other hand and click the camera. The flash brightens the tunnel with intense light. It's a bit brighter for Katie than it is for me, but brightest of all for Koval's more dilated pupils.

In that briefest moment, I see Katie drop and roll right.

I flash the camera again, long enough to see Koval raise his weapon, but I have the jump. I've already aimed. When the bullet hits his left knee, he goes down before he can get off a single round.

I hear the sound of metal against bone. Maglite against skull. When I turn on my phone's flashlight, Katie is standing over Koval, smiling.

I smile back. "Now we're even."

CHAPTER 34

After a debriefing with three different agencies—local police, FBI, and CIA—nothing about my story has changed. Not the part where I, with a lot of help from a few friends, keep a building full of people *and* our national security safe.

Or the part where I'm basically out of the spy business.

As happy as I am about the first half, especially considering it was supposed to end with me on a slab in the morgue if Marchuk had his way, I'm totally bummed about the second. I love being an operative, and just when I figure out I'm pretty damn good at it after all, they take the job away from me. That doesn't mean I won't keep fighting for it.

"But boss, I was never supposed to be in the field anyway," I plead with Rogers, who got on a Company plane the moment she knew Berg had found me safe in that stairwell. So now I get to make my case in person. "Why not put me back on the desk and let me continue hacking?"

"And you'd be happy just hacking?" Rogers asks.

She leans back against the same squad car I was locked inside of three hours ago. I can tell from her expression that she won't believe me, no matter how hard I try to convince her I'll be happy just hacking. I guess that's why she's the boss spy. And she'd be right, because I'd be lying.

"After all this Prettyboy stuff dies down, maybe I could—"

"Exactly what I thought," Rogers interrupts. "I've never met an officer who got a taste of working in the field and wanted to come back to the office. Look, we'll keep you on the payroll long enough to finish the school year and graduate with your friend—what's his name again?"

I laugh when Bunk's real name pops into my head. "We call him Bunker."

"Well, you deserve at least that, a normal senior year, after the great work you've done here." Rogers smiles, but only for a second. "Though you should have told Berg about the hacker, what she looked like. She walked right out of here, free and clear."

It's true. I spotted her on Carlisle's surveillance video during my debriefing with Berg. The time stamp showed that she already had a couple hours' jump on us by then.

"I tried to tell Berg about the hacker," I argue.

"You should have tried harder," Rogers says in a tone that suggests she's about done hearing my case. "Just take my offer to finish school and be happy about it."

"Okay, I accept," I say, as though I have a choice. "But I want normal only for the next seven months. People have the attention span of a gnat. By the time I graduate, people will have forgotten—"

"Sorry, Peter, we can't take that risk for you or other operatives," Rogers says, and I know she's right. "Your face is just too recognizable for covert ops in the intelligence business. But you're the best hacker I've ever worked with. I'll find you something in another agency. They're always looking for people at the IRS."

I laugh until I realize she's serious. "You mean the tax people? I'm a hacker, not a number cruncher."

"Don't mock them. Their criminal investigations unit took down Al Capone when no one else could."

I let it go, mostly because Rogers isn't hearing any of it, but also because there are worse places to be a suspended CIA operative. For a down-and-out hacker trying to prove his way back into the Company, Colorado is paradise with all the federal agencies here I can crack. Or spy on, for the team. NORAD is just down the road, and there's nearby New Mexico and all the labs down there working on serious top-secret stuff. Which reminds me.

"What about the hacker? Sveta Koval isn't the type to retire just because her brother and old boss are in prison. She'll resurface. I could track her down just like I did before and—"

"And *nothing*, Smith, unless you want me to fire you today," Rogers threatens before leaving me so she can help Berg and Jones deal with the throng of media that has gathered in front of Carlisle.

The Internal Revenue Service. Despite what Rogers said about Al Capone, I imagine a life filled with tax returns and paper shuffling. It's depressing.

"Don't look so down," says a voice from behind me. "You're a hero, Prettyboy."

It's a good thing Katie is the one who says it, because I have vowed to knock out the next person to call me that.

"Better get used to it if you plan on staying at Carlisle. Or even in this country. Look," she says, pointing to the crowd outside the line of parked police cars that Berg is using to create a Maginot Line for the media. "Those girls should be at home in the arms of their parents, or at least having a Netflix binge, after the day they've had, but they came back to cheer for you."

"A few hours ago, a couple of them were part of the library posse trying to give me up to Koval."

"Well, people do crazy things when they're under duress."

I wonder if she's talking about what she said to me when we both thought we were about to die, about being my girlfriend. But instead of asking, I just follow her as she starts walking down the long driveway away from the crowd. We're quiet for a few minutes as we climb the ridge and start heading down again toward Carlisle's gated entrance and the main road.

"They love me for now. I only have to wait until a prettier boy goes viral."

"A prettier boy? There can be no other," Katie says, trying to sound like Hollywood Voice-over Guy. "Not that I think you're pretty."

"Way to make me feel better."

"No. I mean that isn't how I'd describe you."

She looks over at me like she's just seeing me for the first time. And I know she isn't seeing a CIA operative, or even Peter Smith. Katie sees only me—Jake Morrow. The guy who is crazy about her.

"I think ruggedly handsome is more appropriate," she continues, and I wonder if she can tell I'm grinning inside.

"Pretty boys have never been my thing. I like to be the only pretty one in the relationship and I'm not ashamed to say it."

I think Katie just said what I've wanted to hear since I first met her at new student orientation. So I want to make sure I heard right.

"Is that what we are—in a relationship?"

"I don't know." She looks off toward the mountains, like she's really thinking it through. "It'll be hard with you staying here and me being shipped off to . . . well, you know . . ."

"I know. That's classified."

Katie stops on the side of the drive, near the oddly placed shed. Seeing it sends a shiver of dread through me, but it goes away the minute Katie takes my hand and asks, "But we're in something, wouldn't you say?"

I remember the question I asked her earlier, and how she never gave me a direct answer.

"Are you sure you didn't know who I was when I asked you out? Because the way you kissed me . . . I mean, after the movie, in your car—"

For a moment, I think she's about to kiss me again, right now. Maybe I'm projecting, because I've been wait-ing weeks to put my arms around her again, but her expression says that's all she wants to do. But she only holds her hand to my cheek for a second, like we're in some movie. Why do girls do that? Don't they know a kiss would be so much more effective at getting the guy? I mean, I've already been got, but still.

"I told you. I don't lie. At least, I won't lie to you ever again. I knew you were a guy who—for the three hours we were on the date, at least—made me forget I was on a mission. Made me forget I am a covert operative, forget all the bad I've seen. With you, Petah Smith, I was just a girl who really liked a boy."

"Yeah?"

"I mean *really* liked," Katie says, moving closer to me.

I move in closer, too. "Then you should probably call me Jake Morrow."

I'm just about to kiss her when a voice stops me cold.

"She should probably call you dead."

So Blondie isn't in the wind after all. When I turn around, I expect to find her armed with a rifle or something, but she's holding a phone. By now, I know that in Sveta Koval's hands, a phone is never just a phone.

"At least you'll die at the hands of your own government," she says. "Sort of. I hacked an armed drone that was on training maneuvers at Buckley Air Force Base."

At that moment, I hear a buzzing noise and look up to see a drone coming over the ridge, aiming right for Katie and me. I instinctively reach for my sidearm, but Rogers took it away. We're exposed, unarmed, and out in the open. The nearest cover is the stand of Russian olive trees, too far away to be any help.

Two targets are harder to hit than one, and I know Sveta wants me more than Katie. If Sveta sends her drone after me, Katie might have time to reach those trees. I grab her hand, squeeze, then let it go.

"Run, Katie!"

Just as Katie takes off running, I hear a car come over the ridge, followed by a loud thump. I turn back in time to see Sveta on the car's hood, her phone flying through the air. No longer under her control, the drone falls to the ground. The car screeches to a stop and Sveta slides off and onto the ground, moaning. For a brief moment, I regret that she's still alive.

Bunker jumps out of the car, looking almost as horrified as he did when Sveta had the rifle in his back. That memory makes me not want to call an ambulance for her crazy ass.

"Did I kill her?"

"No, unfortunately," Katie says. "You didn't hit her quite hard enough. But it will definitely sting for a while."

"I didn't mean to, I swear. I just came over the hill and there she was."

I try to shake off the adrenaline rush from almost dying for the umpteenth time today. "You saved our lives, man."

"I really wasn't trying to hit her at all," Bunker says, sounding freaked out. "I just thought maybe you'd want a ride home, so I came back for you."

I pick up Sveta's phone before going over to her and checking her injuries. There is no visible blood, but the less-evolved part of me can hope for a little internal bleeding. She's still moaning, but her heart rate is good and her skin isn't clammy, which means she probably isn't in shock.

"She'll be fine, Bunk. She's like a roach—nearly impossible to eradicate. Keep an eye on her while I call Rogers to get an EMT and a police escort."

"I'll call." Bunker takes my phone and nods behind me, where a black SUV is pulling through the gate.

I'm worried there's another hostile on the loose because, as everyone knows, covert operatives only travel in black SUVs. But Katie waves at it, and I realize it's come for her.

I want to smash something or someone for a million reasons: Rogers for basically firing me, MI6 for taking Katie away, Sveta for ruining *everything*.

Then Katie comes over and kisses me and I damn near forget about Sveta, Rogers, and the entire universe. I hold her like it will be the last time. She kisses me again like it's only a preview of more to come.

Now she's smiling at me like we share a secret.

"See? Told you I wasn't lying. When your fifteen minutes of fame are done, call me. We're always looking for exceptional talent."

Katie just offered me her heart and a job. My girl is awesome.

She looks at me like she never wants to leave. In my head, I tell her I don't ever want her to. We stand there for a second before she breaks away and gets into the SUV, and they drive off.

So she doesn't hear me when I say, "I'll do that. Then I'll owe you one."

About the Author

Kimberly Reid prepared early for life as a writer of criminals, sleuths, and international spies—even if she didn't realize it back then. She lucked into a family that works in police departments, courtrooms, and as private investigators. She attended a high school focused on international relations and later studied national security policy in college. Now Kimberly lives in Colorado and writes stories about all of those things. Learn more at www.kimberlyreid .com.